P9-CCW-947

THE CHRISTMAS PIG

Also by J.K. Rowling

Harry Potter and the Sorcerer's Stone
Harry Potter and the Chamber of Secrets
Harry Potter and the Prisoner of Azkaban
Harry Potter and the Goblet of Fire
Harry Potter and the Order of the Phoenix
Harry Potter and the Half-Blood Prince
Harry Potter and the Deathly Hallows

Fantastic Beasts and Where to Find Them
Quidditch Through the Ages
(Published in aid of Comic Relief and Lumos)

The Tales of Beedle the Bard
(Published in aid of Lumos)

Harry Potter and the Cursed Child
(Based on an original story by J.K. Rowling,
John Tiffany, and Jack Thorne.
A play by Jack Thorne.)

Fantastic Beasts and Where to Find Them (The Original Screenplay)
Fantastic Beasts: The Crimes of Grindelwald (The Original Screenplay)

The Ickabog

J.K. ROWLING

THE CHRISTMAS PIG

ILLUSTRATED BY JIM FIELD

SCHOLASTIC INC.

Library of Congress Control Number: 2021938338

ISBN 978-1-338-79023-8

10 9 8 7 6 5 4 3 2 1   21 22 23 24 25

Printed in the U.S.A. 12

First edition, October 2021

Art direction by Sophie Stericker and David Saylor
Book design by Charles Kreloff

The text was set in Goudy Old Style, a typeface designed by Frederic W. Goudy.
The display type was set in Charcuterie Contrast, a typeface designed by Laura Worthington.

The artwork was created in pencil and digital.

To David
— J.K. Rowling

For Sandy and Lola
— Jim Field

CONTENTS

Part One

DUR PIG

Part Two

MISLAID

Part Three

DISPOSABLE

Part Four

BOTHER-IT'S-GONE

Part Five

THE WASTES OF THE UNLAMENTED

Part Six

THE CITY OF THE MISSED

Part Seven

THE ISLAND OF THE BELOVED

Part Eight

THE LOSER'S LAIR

Part Nine

HOME

Part One
DUR PIG

DUR PIG

Dur Pig was a small toy pig made of the same material as a soft towel. He had little plastic beans in his tummy, which made him fun to throw. His squishy trotters were exactly the right size to wipe away a tear. When his owner, Jack, was very young, he fell asleep every night sucking Dur Pig's ear.

Dur Pig got his name because when Jack started to talk, he said "dur pig" instead of "the pig." When new, Dur Pig had been salmony-pink, with shiny black plastic eyes, but Jack couldn't remember Dur Pig looking like that. Dur Pig had surely always been as he was now: grayish and faded, with one ear stiff from all the sucking. Dur Pig's eyes fell out, leaving tiny holes in his face for a while, but then Jack's mum, who was a nurse, sewed little buttons in place of the missing plastic beads. When Jack came home from nursery that afternoon, Dur Pig was lying on the kitchen table wrapped up in a woolen scarf, waiting for Jack to take off the little bandage covering his eyes. Mum had even made Dur Pig a set of medical notes: "DP Jones. Operation to attach buttons. Surgeon: Mum."

CHAPTER 1

After his eye operation, everyone started calling Dur Pig "DP" for short. From the time he was two years old, Jack would never go to bed without DP, which often caused problems, because when bedtime came, DP was usually nowhere to be found. Sometimes it took Mum and Dad a long time to find DP, who turned up in all kinds of places: hiding inside one of Dad's shoes or scrunched up in a flowerpot.

"Why d'you keep hiding him, Jack?" Mum asked every time she found DP curled up in a kitchen drawer or hidden beneath a sofa cushion.

The answer was private, between Jack and DP. Jack knew DP liked cozy spaces where he could snuggle up and sleep.

DP liked doing exactly the same things Jack did: crawling under bushes and into hidey-holes and being thrown up in the air, Jack by his Dad, and DP by Jack. DP didn't mind getting dirty, or being dropped accidentally in a puddle, as long as he and Jack were having fun together.

Once, when Jack was three, he put DP in the recycling bin. When he'd heard Mum say the bin was for recycling, Jack thought it had something to do with bike rides, so he waited for Mum to leave the kitchen, then dropped DP in there, imagining he'd have a little spin around when the lid was on. Mum laughed when Jack explained why he was peeking in the bin to try and catch the things moving. She explained that "recycling" meant something very different to going for a bike ride. All the things in the bin were going to be taken away and turned into other things, so they'd have a whole new life. Jack definitely didn't want DP to go away and be changed into something else, so he never put DP in the recycling bin again.

All his adventures gave DP his interesting smell, which Jack liked very much. It was a mixture of the places DP had gone on his adventures, along with the warm dark cave under Jack's blankets, and just a trace of Mum's perfume, because she always hugged and kissed DP, too, when she came to say good night to Jack.

Every now and then, Mum would decide DP had gotten a bit too smelly and needed a good clean. The first time DP ever went in the washing machine, Jack had lain on the kitchen floor and screamed with rage and fear. Mum had tried to show Jack how much DP was enjoying swirling around in the washing machine, but it wasn't until DP was back in the cave under Jack's blankets that night, soft and dry and smelling of washing powder, that Jack really forgave Mum. He soon got used to DP going in the washing machine, but he always looked forward to DP returning to his natural smell.

The very worst that ever happened to DP was when Jack was four, and lost him at the beach. Dad had already packed up the towels and Mum was helping Jack back into his sweatshirt, when Jack suddenly remembered burying DP somewhere, though he couldn't quite remember where. They searched until the sun was setting and the beach was almost empty, and Dad got really cross, and Jack wailed and sobbed, but Mum kept telling him not to give up hope, and digging all round with her hands. Then, just as Dad was saying they'd have to leave without DP, Jack dug his bare foot into the sand and his toes hit something squashy. Jack pulled DP out, sobbing with happiness, and Dad said that DP was never to come to the beach again, which Jack thought very unfair, because DP loved sand, which was why Jack had buried him in the first place.

MUM AND DAD

Shortly before Jack started school, a letter arrived telling all the parents that the children should bring their favorite cuddly toy with them on their first day. Everybody in Jack's class brought a teddy, but Jack, of course, brought DP. Each child took his or her turn to walk up to the front of the class and explain what their cuddly toy's name was, and why they liked it. When it was Jack's turn, he explained why DP was called "DP," and about the operation on his eyes, and about the day he got buried on the beach and was nearly lost forever. The stories of DP and his adventures made the class laugh and when Jack finished talking, they all clapped. DP was easily the funniest and most interesting toy, even though he was one of the shabbiest. At playtime, Jack and a boy called Freddie played catch with DP. Just before the end of break, Jack dropped DP in a puddle. That night, DP had to go in the washing machine again.

If Jack ever had a bad day at school—if he got a low mark, or had an argument with Freddie, or if somebody made fun of Jack's wonky clay pot—DP was waiting at home to wipe away a tear with his small, squishy trotters. Whatever happened to Jack, DP was there, understanding and forgiving, and carrying with him that comforting smell of home, which always came back, no matter how often Mum washed it off.

One night, soon after he'd started school, a noise woke Jack up. He felt for DP and drew him close in the dark.

Somebody was shouting. The voice was a bit like Dad's. Then there was a crash and a lady screamed: it sounded like Mum, but not as Jack had ever heard her. Jack was scared. He listened for a few more moments, pressing DP against his mouth and nose, and he knew DP was scared, too.

Jack thought Mum and Dad might be fighting a burglar together. He knew the number you had to call for the police, so he got out of bed in the dark and crept out onto the landing. Still holding DP, he tiptoed downstairs. Dad was still yelling and Mum was still screaming. Jack couldn't hear the burglar's voice.

Then the sitting room door banged open and Dad strode into the hall. He wasn't wearing his pajamas, but jeans and a sweatshirt. Dad didn't notice Jack on the stairs. He opened the front door, walked out, and slammed it behind him. Jack heard the noise of the car engine in the drive. Dad drove away.

Jack crept into the sitting room. The lamp was on the floor and Mum was sitting on the sofa with her face in her hands, crying. When she heard Jack's footsteps, she looked up, startled, then cried harder than ever. Jack thought she'd explain everything and make it all better, but when he ran to her, she only hugged him very close, the way he held DP when he was hurt or sad.

CHANGES

Dad didn't live with them anymore after that.

Mum and Dad explained to Jack separately that they didn't want to be married anymore. Jack told them he understood. He said that other people at school had mums and dads who didn't live together. He could tell that they needed him to be all right about it all, so he pretended he was.

But some nights, after Mum had kissed him and closed the door, Jack cried into DP's limp body. DP knew and understood everything without being told. He knew about the hard lump in Jack's chest. His trotters wiped away Jack's tears. Jack didn't have to pretend in the dark with DP.

Soon after Jack's sixth birthday, Dad took Jack out for a burger, gave him a big box of LEGOs, and explained that he'd gotten a job abroad.

"I can talk to you all the time, though, Jack," said Dad. "You can fly on an airplane to visit me. It'll be fun, won't it?"

Jack didn't think it sounded nearly as much fun as having a dad around to play with, but he didn't say that. Jack was getting used to not saying things.

Next, Mum told him it might be a good idea if they moved to be closer to Gran and Grandpa, who could take care of Jack when she needed to work late. She had a new job at a big hospital, and Grandpa had found them a lovely house with a garden, just two streets away from Gran and Grandpa's house. Gran and Grandpa owned a very naughty dog called Toby. Jack found Toby-the-dog funny.

"But will I have to leave school?" asked Jack, thinking of his best friend, Freddie.

"Yes," said Mum, "but there's a school very near our new house. I know you'll love it."

"I don't think I will," said Jack.

He didn't want to move and he didn't want a new school. Mum didn't seem to understand: Jack didn't want any more changes. He wanted to stay with his school friends and in the old house, where he and DP had had so many adventures.

Gran and Grandpa talked to Jack on the phone. They told him how much they were looking forward to him and Mum coming to live near them, and what fun they'd have playing with Toby-the-dog in the park. So Jack said it was all right, but he didn't really mean it. The only person who seemed to understand was DP. Jack knew DP would miss all their favorite hiding places, too.

A few weeks after Mum had told Jack about the new house, Jack said goodbye to his teacher and Freddie. The next day, the removal men came and took away everything that made the old house look like home, and Mum drove Jack and DP a hundred miles in their car.

Jack had to admit the journey was fun. DP sat on Jack's lap, and Mum and Jack played I Spy and stopped for pizza and ice cream halfway. Mum let Jack buy two gobstoppers out of the gumball machine, one for him and one for DP (although, as Jack explained to Mum back in the car, he'd have to eat DP's for him).

He hadn't expected to, but Jack liked the new house. His bedroom was next to Mum's and there was a tall tree outside his window. Gran and Grandpa arrived five minutes after they did, with bags of food to fill up the fridge. The first thing Toby-the-dog did was to try and snatch DP out of Jack's hand.

"No, Toby, you know DP's mine!" said Jack. He shoved DP down the front of his sweatshirt to keep him safe, but with his head sticking out so DP could see what was going on.

The removal men lifted all their familiar furniture into the house. Mum and Gran put away all the kitchen things while Jack, Grandpa, Toby-the-dog, and DP explored the garden. It had lots of interesting hiding places and excellent high perches for DP, but Jack kept him close, because he didn't trust Toby-the-dog not to try and snatch him again.

That night, Jack held DP in bed, breathing in his familiar comforting smell, and they silently agreed that moving day hadn't been nearly as bad as Jack had expected. There were no curtains on Jack's window yet, and DP and Jack watched the leaves fluttering against the darkening sky outside, before they fell asleep.

HOLLY MACAULAY

When Monday arrived, Mum caught Jack trying to sneak DP into his schoolbag.

"No, Jack," she said gently. "What if he got lost?"

The thought of DP getting lost at a new school among strangers was dreadful, so Jack put DP back in his bedroom, but he felt very lonely and frightened as he approached the school gates.

"I'm sure you'll have a lovely day," said Mum, hugging him before the bell rang and he had to go inside.

Jack didn't say anything. He was frowning with the effort it took not to look scared.

The children in his new class all stared at him. They seemed bigger than the people in his old class. The teacher spoke to him kindly and asked his name. Then she asked the rest of the class to come to the front one by one, to show what they'd collected for the nature topic. Jack didn't have anything, of course, so he watched while people showed leaves, acorns, and conkers to the class.

Then came break time. Jack found a corner where nobody would bother him.

After break, the teacher told everybody to take out their reading books. She gave one to Jack. Then she told the children that today was a special day, because some older students were visiting the class. Everybody would get a partner who'd help them with their reading.

The classroom door opened and in came lots of big children from the top year. They were all grinning and a few of them waved at younger children whom they knew. Jack felt more scared than ever.

One tall girl stood out from the rest. She had long black hair, which she'd tied back in a ponytail. She wasn't giggling behind her hand like a lot of the other big girls. She stood calmly while the teacher invited the older children to pick a partner. When the tall girl caught Jack's eye, he quickly examined his fingers.

The big children began moving among the desks and Jack's classmates all began whispering, "Holly! Holly! Over here, Holly!"

The girl sitting beside Jack was whispering, "Holly! Holly!" too.

When she saw Jack looking at her, the girl next to him explained, "See her, with the long black hair? That's Holly Macaulay. She's a really good gymnast. She's been on TV."

"Hello," said a voice a long way above Jack's head.

He looked up. Holly Macaulay, who'd been on TV, was looking down at him.

"You're new, aren't you?" she said.

Jack tried to say yes but his voice wouldn't work. Everyone was staring at him, and the frantic whispers of "Holly, Holly, Holly, over here!" became louder than ever.

But Holly Macaulay ignored all of them. She pulled up a chair and sat down beside Jack.

"I'm going to be *your* partner," she said.

It might seem strange to compare a floppy little pig to a tall eleven-year-old girl who'd been on TV, but not to Jack. DP had brought him friends on his very first day at his old school, and Holly Macaulay did the same for him at his new school. After just one hour with Holly as his reading partner, Jack was no longer the quiet new boy. He was the boy Holly Macaulay had chosen, the boy Holly Macaulay called "my mate Jack" when she saw him at the packed lunch table later.

The rest of his class was impressed. They wanted to talk to him now. After he'd finished his sandwiches at lunchtime, a boy called Rory asked Jack if he wanted to play football. Rory knew lots of good jokes. When Mum picked Jack up at the end of the day, Rory tugged his mum over to Jack's mum, and the two mothers made arrangements for Jack to go and play at Rory's house later in the week.

DP was delighted Jack had had such a good first day at his new school. He loved hearing about Holly Macaulay and Rory. Of course, Jack didn't have to say anything out loud. Snuggled under the blankets, with the sound of rustling leaves just outside his window, DP knew and understood everything without being told. Jack fell asleep with DP's bean-filled body against his cheek, his familiar smell mingling with that of the new paint in Jack's room.

HOLLY'S DP

All that term, Jack and Holly remained reading partners. The more he got to know her, the more he understood why his whole class wanted to be her friend.

Apart from being very clever, and always getting top marks, and having a voice good enough to sing solos at assembly, Holly Macaulay was one of the best young gymnasts in the country. She'd been on TV once and in the newspaper twice. It was her ambition to compete in the Olympic Games. Some of this she told Jack herself, the rest he heard from other people.

Holly wasn't bigheaded, even though she was famous. She showed Jack the bruises she got when she fell off the beam. Gymnastics sounded like very hard work. Holly told Jack how she had to win and keep winning. Even getting second place wasn't good enough. She couldn't afford to lose, if she was to get to the Olympics.

Then one day, Holly appeared for their reading lesson looking strange. Her eyes were red and puffy and when she said hello, her voice came out as a croak.

CHAPTER 5

Even though he liked Holly very much, Jack was still a little bit shy with her.

"Did you . . . did you lose?" he whispered. He remembered that Holly had had a big gymnastics competition at the weekend.

She shook her head. "I didn't go."

"Were you ill?" asked Jack.

Again, Holly shook her head.

They read another page of Jack's reading book. Then a big tear splashed onto the page.

"My mum's left my dad," whispered Holly.

Sheltering behind Jack's reading book, she told him everything.

Holly's mum had told her to pack a bag and then driven her away to a flat while Holly's dad was still at work at the hospital. Holly didn't know when she'd next see her dad. She missed him. He was the one who usually took her to gymnastics competitions. Her mum had explained that she didn't love Holly's dad anymore.

"They both want me to live with them," Holly told Jack in a whisper. "I don't know what to do."

After reading hour was over and Holly returned to her own class, Jack wondered what had made her tell him all those secret, private things. Perhaps, he thought, he was like Holly's DP. Even though he hadn't said much, he'd understood.

MORE CHANGES

Jack had gotten used to Dad sending him postcards from all the different cities he visited for work. Mum stuck the postcards on the fridge where Jack could always see them. There was one with bridges over canals, and another of a town set high in the snowy mountains. Jack spoke to Dad by phone and texted him pictures of the drawings he'd done at school and his Level Four swimming certificate. Jack loved swimming. He was one of the best in his class, so he had his seventh birthday party at the pool. Lots of his classmates came, including his best friend, Rory.

Before school broke up for the summer, Holly Macaulay was on television for the second time. She came to the front at assembly to show everyone another gold medal, and the whole school applauded, and she waved and winked at Jack.

Mum and Jack went away to Greece on holiday, with Gran and Grandpa. DP came, too. He loved the sun. His limp little body was bleached a paler shade of gray as he lay on a towel beside Jack by the pool, but Jack remembered not to bury him in the sand again.

CHAPTER 6

When Jack returned to school for the new year, Holly Macaulay had moved up to Big School. He missed seeing her, but he had lots of friends now.

One evening, Gran and Grandpa came over to babysit, because Mum was going out. This was strange, because Mum never usually went out in the evenings. When he asked where she was going, Mum told Jack she was going out for dinner with a friend. She looked pretty. She was wearing a new dress.

After that, Mum went out once a week in the evening. Jack didn't mind. He had fun with Gran and Grandpa, who played board games with him, but he always made sure to put DP up somewhere high when Toby-the-dog was staying the night.

Then, one sunny weekend, Mum told Jack that her friend Brendan was coming over in his car and that the three of them would be going out for the day.

"Is it Brendan you go to dinner with?" Jack asked. Mum said it was.

Brendan turned out to be a friendly looking man with a deep voice. He drove Mum and Jack to a country park where there was an adventure playground. Jack went down the slide and climbed up the rope net, but he wasn't really having much fun. It felt strange not having Mum to himself. After Jack had had enough of the adventure playground, the three of them went for a walk down to the river. Brendan showed Jack how to skim stones over the water. Jack would much rather it had been Dad teaching him.

After Brendan had driven them home and said goodbye, Mum asked whether Jack liked Brendan. Jack said he was quite nice.

They went out a lot with Brendan after that. Jack could tell that Mum really liked Brendan. Once he came back from the swings and saw them holding hands on a bench, but Mum quickly let go when she realized Jack had seen.

Beneath the blankets, DP understood everything without being told. He knew Jack felt strange about Brendan holding Mum's hand, even though Jack liked Brendan a bit more, now that he'd gotten to know him. DP understood that Jack would rather it had been his dad holding Mum's hand. DP shared Jack's worry that if Brendan stopped wanting to be Mum's friend anymore, she'd get sad again. DP was the only one Jack could tell how much he wanted things to stop changing. He never needed to pretend with DP.

NOT JACK'S DAD

Jack knew that Brendan—like Mum—had been married before, and that he had a daughter. Some weekends Brendan didn't see Mum because his daughter came to stay with him and he was busy doing things with her.

One day, Mum announced that the four of them were going to go to the cinema together: Mum, Jack, Brendan, and his daughter, Holly.

"*Holly?*" said Jack.

And sure enough, there she was: Holly Macaulay, taller than ever now and much older looking than Jack remembered. There was another change, too. Though he was so pleased to see Holly, she didn't seem very pleased to see Jack. She was polite to Mum but when Mum asked her about her gymnastics, Holly only said yes and no. She wouldn't let Mum help her with anything, and when Mum asked her if she wanted to go to the bathroom, she said she was old enough to go by herself, thanks very much. Jack didn't like

Holly being rude to his mum. It was the first time he'd ever seen Holly be nasty to anyone.

Talking it over later with DP in bed (they weren't really talking, of course, but it came to the same thing, because DP understood everything Jack thought), Jack supposed that Holly found it odd to see her dad with another lady. All the same, his mum was lovely. Holly shouldn't talk to her like that.

Nearly a year after Brendan had taught Jack to skim stones over the water, Mum said that she had something to tell Jack. She looked nervous. She was hiding her left hand in her lap.

"Brendan has asked me to marry him," she said.

"Oh," said Jack.

He thought for a bit.

"Will he come and live with us?"

"Yes," said Mum, still looking nervous. "Do you mind, Jack?"

Jack liked Brendan a lot better now. Brendan had taught him to play checkers, and helped him with his homework. All the same, he didn't see why they couldn't keep things as they were.

"Will I have to call him 'Dad'?"

"No," said Mum. "Your dad is 'Dad.' You can keep calling Brendan, 'Brendan.'"

"Do Gran and Grandpa know?" asked Jack. He secretly hoped Gran and Grandpa might not be happy about it, but Mum said they liked Brendan very much, and were glad.

"Will Holly be my sister?"

"Your stepsister," said Mum. "You like Holly, don't you?"

CHAPTER 7

"Yes," said Jack.

It was sort of true. He'd never forgotten how kind Holly had been to him when he'd first come to school. Sometimes she was a lot of fun, but at other times she could be sharp and sarcastic. Mum said it was because she was a teenager.

Mum and Brendan got married in a registry office in late summer. Jack had to wear a suit, because he was the ring bearer. Holly was bridesmaid and wore a blue dress, with cornflowers in her long hair.

Afterward, they all went to a restaurant. Brendan's mum and dad came. They were very kind to Jack and got on well with Gran and Grandpa. Everybody seemed happy, although Holly didn't talk much.

"She's got a big competition next week," said Brendan, putting his arm around Holly in her bridesmaid's dress. "We're all going to go and cheer her on."

"Who's 'we'?" asked Holly.

"Judy and Jack could come, too," said Brendan. Judy was Jack's mum's name.

"I don't want them to come," said Holly. Her eyes had filled with tears. "I want you to come on your own, like always."

There was a little silence at the table and then everybody talked loudly at once.

Much later in the evening, one of Brendan's friends played the piano and the grown-ups danced. Jack felt sleepy. He wanted his bed and DP.

Then Holly sat down beside him at the table. She spoke in a low, fierce voice.

"He's not your dad," she said. "He's mine. Just because he lives with you doesn't make him your dad. Understand?"

Holly's expression scared Jack a bit.

"Yes," he said. "I understand."

THE TOILET ROLL ANGEL

From then on, Holly spent alternate weekends at their house. Jack never knew whether she was going to be kind Holly or mean Holly. He and Mum were never allowed to watch Holly do her gymnastics. They were barely allowed to ask her how competitions went.

When Holly was in a good mood, she'd play video games with Jack and football in the back garden. At other times—especially if she'd lost a competition—she could be really horrible. Once, she called him a stupid baby when she saw him cuddling DP. Jack felt ashamed, and after that, he hid DP whenever Holly was coming to stay.

Brendan told Jack that Holly was having to work twice as hard to win at competitions, because a new girl had moved into their area who was nearly as good as Holly.

Jack tried his best not to annoy Holly when she came to spend the weekend, but it was hard to know what would set her off. When Jack had a cold, she shouted at him for sniffing during her favorite TV program. When Brendan told her off, Holly stormed out of the room, slamming the door behind her. Brendan ran after her. After sitting on his own for a bit, Jack decided to go upstairs to his bedroom. He curled up on his bed with DP, who silently agreed that it wasn't Jack's fault he'd sniffed, and that Holly had been horrible.

It was nearly Christmas. School broke up. Jack was excited because he'd asked for a new bike and so had his best friend, Rory. There was a good paved bit of play-park near Rory's house and he and Jack were planning to race their new bikes there.

When Mum took out the box of Christmas decorations that year, she showed Brendan the angel that had always sat on top of their family tree. Jack had made it when he was in nursery school. The angel's body was a toilet roll, its wings were made of card with glitter glued on, and it had a beard made of brown wool.

"Angels don't have beards!" said Holly scornfully, when she saw Jack's creation on top of the tree. Mum and Brendan were in the kitchen when Holly said this. "Why would anyone put an old toilet roll on a Christmas tree? My mum wouldn't put up stuff I'd made when I was a *baby*. She'd know I'd be embarrassed."

Jack suddenly remembered how Dad always used to say "and now for the finishing touch," and lift Jack up so he could put the toilet roll angel on the tree, last of all. For a moment, Jack wanted his dad to come home so badly it gave him a pain in his chest.

This was the last time Jack was going to see Holly before

Christmas, because Holly's mum was taking her away to visit relatives abroad. Jack was glad. If he couldn't have Dad, at least he'd have Mum, Brendan, Gran, Grandpa, and Toby-the-dog in a good mood, because Holly wouldn't be slamming doors and forcing the grown-ups to try and keep her happy.

The day before Christmas Eve, Gran came over to look after Jack, because Mum and Brendan were both at work. It had started to snow. Flakes drifted past the window while Jack watched a Christmas movie with DP on his lap. The Christmas tree lights were twinkling in the corner, Toby-the-dog was asleep on the floor, and Jack felt relaxed and happy. He didn't notice the taxi rolling up outside the house.

The doorbell rang. Toby-the-dog jumped up and started barking. Jack heard Gran open the front door and then her exclamation of surprise.

"Holly! What are you doing here?"

Jack looked round in time to see Holly dragging a suitcase into the hall. She looked furious and her cheeks were tearstained.

"I thought you'd be on the plane by now!" said Gran.

"I'm not going!" said Holly. "I want to see Dad!"

"But he's at work, dear," said Gran, bewildered. "Where's your mum?"

Gran peered out into the snowy front garden, but there was nobody there. Holly had come to their house alone.

"I'm not going with her!" shouted Holly, and she stomped toward the stairs, dragging her heavy suitcase with her, and refused to answer any more of Gran's questions.

Gran phoned Brendan, who left work early, and then Holly's mum arrived. Her name was Natalia. Jack had never met her before. He went and hid in his bedroom, but he could still hear what everyone was shouting. It seemed Holly had lost a big gymnastics competition, and her mum had told her it was because she kept missing practices, and Holly had gotten very angry and run away from her mum at the airport.

"I suppose *you* encouraged this!" he heard Natalia shouting at Brendan.

Natalia finally left the house, crying. Holly had refused to go with her, insisting that she wanted to spend Christmas with her dad. Jack was now very hungry, but he didn't want to go downstairs until Mum was there.

By the time Mum came home, Jack was fast asleep on his bed, DP clutched in his hand.

CHRISTMAS EVE

Jack woke up on Christmas Eve holding DP as usual. For a few moments he lay quite still, thinking about the new bike he'd be getting the next day and feeling excited. He knew Mum would have already left for work, and that she had to work late this evening, but she had all of Christmas Day and Boxing Day off.

Then he remembered that Holly was still here. He'd only just had time to wonder what she'd find to get angry about today when there was an enormous crash from downstairs and Toby-the-dog started barking. Jack got up and went to see what had happened.

When he entered the sitting room, he saw the Christmas tree lying on the floor beside an overturned chair. Gran was trying to catch Toby-the-dog, who was ferreting through the decorations in search of all the chocolate ones he shouldn't eat.

"I was only trying to put my decoration on the tree!" Holly was saying, half-sorry, half-defiant. She was holding an ornament she'd made at school and which she'd been attempting to hang near the top. Apparently, she'd lost her balance, seized the tree, and pulled it right over.

"It's all right, dear," said Gran. "No harm done."

But there *was* harm done. When all the baubles that weren't broken were put back on the tree, they realized that the toilet roll angel was missing. Finally, Grandpa found a few wet bits of cardboard and wool: Toby-the-dog had torn the angel apart.

"That blasted dog!" said Grandpa.

Jack knew Mum would be really upset. She loved his angel. Nobody even told Holly off.

"I tell you what we'll do," said Gran, trying to keep things cheerful. "We'll all drive into town and choose a new angel!"

Holly could hardly refuse, seeing as it was her fault the angel had been eaten, but Jack could tell she really didn't want to go. She sat scowling on the sofa and texting her friends. When Jack went upstairs to put on his coat, he sneaked DP into his pocket. He felt the need for comfort just now.

THE NEW ANGEL

Holly sat hunched up beside Jack in the back seat of the car, still texting all the way into town.

"Look at all this snow!" said Gran cheerfully as white flecks began to build up on the windscreen and Grandpa switched on the wipers. "Wouldn't a white Christmas be lovely?"

Neither Jack nor Holly said anything.

The pavements in town were covered in brown slush. Christmas music was playing in all the shops and there was a chestnut seller on the corner. Jack held Gran's hand, with his other in his pocket, keeping hold of DP. Crowds bustled around them, all doing last-minute shopping.

They went into a busy department store. There weren't many Christmas decorations left and they looked higgledy-piggledy because shoppers were picking them up and putting them down in a hurry.

"Here's a lovely angel," said Gran, grabbing the first one she saw.

Jack didn't like the angel at all. He thought she was too fancy for their tree. She wore a gaudy purple dress trimmed with gold braid and had large plastic gold wings. Jack didn't think Mum would like her, either. She'd loved his toilet roll angel with the woolly beard.

"What do you think of her, Holly?" Gran asked, but Holly shrugged rudely and kept looking at her phone.

Gran didn't ask Jack. She led them to the checkout desk and bought the angel. Then they headed back to the car park through the cold slush and the bustling crowds.

On the way back home in the car, Holly said, "I feel sick."

"Maybe you should stop texting while we're in the car, dear," said Gran.

Holly rolled her eyes and pressed the button to lower the window. An icy blast filled the back of the car and flecks of snow swept inside.

"I'm cold," said Jack.

"I need fresh air," snapped Holly.

They reached the motorway. Jack was now shivering. He felt miserable and angry. Why did Holly always have to have things her way?

"Gran, I'm cold."

"Holly, close the window a bit, please," said Gran.

Holly put the window up a fraction. Sleet and snow continued to blow into the car.

"It's still wide open," said Jack.

Holly stuck out her lower lip, making a baby face, and pointed at DP, whom Jack had pulled out of his pocket. Grandpa saw her do it in his rearview mirror.

"Enough of that, miss," he said. "Wind up the window, please."

Holly scowled and put the window up another bit. Then she turned to Jack, stuck out her bottom lip again, and pretended to be a baby rubbing tears from its eyes.

Jack didn't believe Holly really felt sick. She just wanted to be nasty. She was ruining Christmas Eve and she'd probably ruin Christmas Day, too, snapping at Jack and making herself the center of attention. She kept silently taunting him with the baby face. The hard, tight ball of anger in Jack's tummy burned suddenly red hot.

"Loser," he whispered.

Holly stopped making the baby face at once.

"Shut up," she growled.

Jack didn't care that he'd made her even angrier. She was ruining everything. She was rude to Mum, Gran, and Grandpa. She'd come to stay when he didn't want her. It was all her fault Toby-the-dog had eaten his bearded angel. He wanted to punish her for spoiling Christmas and he knew exactly how to do it. There was nothing Holly hated in the world more than losing.

"Loser," said Jack, more loudly.

"Jack," said Grandpa sharply from the driver's seat, "I hope you didn't just say what I think you said."

Jack didn't answer. He could tell that Holly was on the verge of tears now, and he was glad. He was sick of her bullying. He didn't care about keeping the peace. He'd had no dinner last night because of Holly. He was tired of having to tiptoe around her.

She suddenly pressed the window button, lowering it all the way to the bottom again, so that an icy gale blew through the car.

"Holly—" began Gran.

"I'm going to be sick!" said Holly. Jack knew she was doing it in revenge. So he did something that he'd seen people do at school: they used their thumbs and forefingers to make an L shape and held it up to their foreheads. The "L" stood for "loser."

He made the L shape, held it up, and glared at Holly.

So fast that he had no hope of stopping her, Holly leaned forward, seized DP out of Jack's lap, and threw him out of the open window. For a brief second, Jack saw DP frozen against the steely sky, his little trotters spread-eagled; then he was whipped away out of sight.

LOST

Jack yelled so loudly that Grandpa swerved dangerously.

"She threw DP out of the window!" bellowed Jack. "*She threw DP out of the window!*"

But Grandpa couldn't stop in the middle of the motorway. They drove on for what seemed like ages before he was able to pull over. Holly's arms were folded, her face was cold and set. She didn't seem to care at all about what she'd done. Once they'd stopped, Grandpa got out of the car, and ran back the way they'd come, disappearing into the snow, in the hope of rescuing DP.

"Grandpa will find him," said Gran, but Jack didn't believe her. He tried to get out of the car to look for DP himself, but Gran made him stay inside. Jack began to yell and cry. He had to have DP back. DP was the only one in the whole world who knew everything, who always cared and never changed. He needed DP, he *had* to have him, and DP needed Jack, because only the two of them understood each other, and now DP was lying lost on the motorway, believing Jack had left him forever. Jack kicked the back of the driver's seat, still yelling in rage, and tried to punch Holly.

"Jack!" said Gran, shocked. "Calm down! We'll find DP!"

A police car drew up and parked behind them. The policeman got out and came to ask Gran why they'd stopped. Gran explained and the police went away again. Still Grandpa didn't come back. Cars whizzed past, more snow fell, and Jack looked out of the back window, sobbing. He couldn't get rid of the image of DP flying out of the car window, small and floppy and frightened as he cartwheeled away through the air. Grandpa had to find him. He *had* to.

But when Grandpa came back to the car, he gave a little shake of the head as he looked into Gran's eyes, then turned to Jack and said, "I'm sorry, lad. I think he's gone."

After that, Jack was shouting and crying too loudly to hear anything anyone said to him. He couldn't stand feeling the car bearing him away from the place where DP was lying, lost and bewildered and wondering why Jack wasn't coming back for him. They drove home with Jack pummeling his fists against the door of the car, begging to be let out so that he could go back and find DP.

When he got home, Jack tried to run back up the street toward the motorway. Grandpa grabbed him and half dragged, half carried him into the house. Once inside, Jack ran up to his bedroom and began to throw things. He took all the toys he could reach from their shelves and threw them across the room. He ripped posters down from his walls. He pulled out drawers. He even overturned his desk.

Gran came upstairs.

"Jack, stop it! STOP IT! You're usually such a good little boy!"

In answer, Jack picked up his wastepaper bin and threw it at the window. He'd hoped the glass would break, but it didn't.

"That's enough, young man!" roared Grandpa, appearing in the doorway behind Gran. "You just calm down, right now!"

There wasn't much left to throw or break, so instead Jack launched himself facedown on his bed and refused to move or speak. At last, Gran and Grandpa left him alone.

All Jack's life, when he'd gone to bed, he'd reached for DP. He seemed to feel DP right now: his limp little body, his bean-filled belly, his worn trotters, so good for wiping away tears. He could even smell DP's slightly grubby homelike whiff.

"I'll find you, DP," Jack vowed into his tear-soaked pillow. "I'll come back when they're all asleep."

After an hour, when Jack had cried all he could cry, he lay on his bed in his wrecked room and listened to the sounds of the house around him. He kept hoping to hear the front door open. If Gran phoned Mum at work and told her what had happened, she'd surely come home early. Mum understood how important DP was. She'd help him look. But the front door didn't open.

Grandpa came and knocked on Jack's bedroom door at one o'clock and asked him if he wanted lunch. Jack shouted no. A little while later, Gran came to his door and asked him if he wanted to come and see the new angel on top of the tree. Jack shouted no even louder. Then he heard the front door open and close. For one happy moment, he thought Mum had come home early, just as he'd hoped, but instead, he heard somebody walking away down the snowy front path. He didn't care who it was, or why they were going. He no longer cared about Christmas. All he cared about was DP.

THE CHRISTMAS PIG

It was nearly teatime when he heard the garden gate creak and footsteps coming back up the path. Hoping it was Mum, he jumped up and looked out of the window, but it was only Grandpa and Holly.

Not long afterward, there was another knock on Jack's bedroom door and it opened.

"Jack," said Grandpa. "Holly's got something she'd like to give you."

Holly's face was puffy and tearstained. Jack sat up on his bed, staring at the brown paper bag in Holly's hand. He could think of only one thing that could make up for what she'd done. They must have gone back to the motorway to look for DP. They must have found him.

CHAPTER 12

For the space of a heartbeat, Jack thought that was exactly what they'd done, because when Holly put her hand in the bag, he heard the rattle of belly beans.

Then hope fled. Holly pulled out a brand-new pig. It was the same size as DP, and made of the same toweling material, but it was plump and smug looking, with sleek salmon-pink skin and shiny black eyes that looked like tiny beetles.

"He's just the same, look," said Grandpa. "Holly's very sorry, Jack. She bought it out of her pocket money for you."

"I *am* sorry, Jack," whispered Holly. "*Really, really sorry.*"

When Jack didn't answer, Grandpa said in a falsely jolly voice, "He's a Christmas Pig. Aren't you, eh?" He took the pig from Holly and made it wave a plump trotter at Jack. "See, Jack? He likes you. Now, why don't you come downstairs with us, eh? We'll have some tea and watch a movie. We'll hang up our stockings together. And don't forget your new bike, Jack! Father Christmas is probably loading it onto his sleigh right now! Come on, lad. Come downstairs, bring the Christmas Pig, and we'll all be friends."

Jack got slowly off the bed and held out a hand for the Christmas Pig. He felt, as Jack had expected, horrible: slippery smooth instead of rough and worn. Jack hated his shiny black eyes and perky pink ears, which ought to be lopsided and gray.

"There's a good boy," said Grandpa.

At these words, Jack went into his worst frenzy yet. They thought a brand-new pig could be the same as DP, which showed how little they understood. DP was the only DP in the world and this new pig was nothing . . . *nothing.* Jack threw the Christmas Pig on the floor and stamped on him, then he picked him up, held him by a trotter, and smashed him again and again into the wardrobe, finally grabbing his head and trying to pull it off.

"Jack!" shouted Grandpa. "That's enough, Jack!"

Holly ran out of the bedroom. Jack chucked the Christmas Pig across the room at the wardrobe, then threw himself back onto the bed, yelling and punching his pillow. Nothing Grandpa said or did would persuade him to come downstairs. He didn't care about hanging up his stocking. He didn't want to be a good boy. He didn't want a new bike. The only thing in the world he wanted was DP.

Much, much later, he heard a commotion downstairs. From what Jack overheard, Toby-the-dog had dragged over the tree again in search of the last bits of chocolate and he appeared to have chewed up the new angel, too. Jack was glad. If he hadn't been so sad and angry, he'd have laughed. He wished he could rip up the whole of Christmas, and then perhaps they'd all understand how he felt knowing DP was lying lost on a motorway.

Gran came upstairs and made him put on his pajamas before bed. Jack only did it so she wouldn't realize what he was planning. He got into bed in the room he'd done his best to destroy, with the posters still screwed up on the floor, the drawers still out of the desk, and the Christmas Pig lying in a heap at the foot of the wardrobe, and pretended he was going to go to sleep. At last, Gran left.

The snow swirled against the blackening sky outside his window while Jack waited for the house to fall completely silent. Normally, he'd be very excited. He'd have hung up his stocking with Mum and left out a carrot for Rudolph—but not this Christmas Eve. To be excited about any of that was to betray DP, who was more important than the whole of Christmas put together.

Once everyone fell asleep, Jack was going to get up again, get dressed, sneak out of the house, return to the motorway, and find his oldest friend.

13

THE NIGHT FOR MIRACLES AND LOST CAUSES

Jack knew that he must have fallen asleep because he woke in pitch darkness. People were talking in his room. He supposed Gran and Grandpa had come to see whether he was all right. He kept his eyes shut, because he wanted them to think he was still sleeping.

"It's never been done," said a worried voice. "I'm not sure it's possible."

"Of course it's possible," said a second voice. "It all depends on the boy, on whether he's brave enough."

"He's very brave, but it's too dangerous," said a third voice, which was old and croaky. "I've been there, many times. I know what I'm talking about."

"I've been there, too," a fourth voice. "Most of us have been there at one time or another."

"I haven't," said a fifth voice, which was slow and deep.

"Well, of course *you* haven't," said the first voice. "You're too big. I'm talking about us little Things."

None of these people sounded familiar. Jack was starting to feel scared. Who were they? He didn't want to open his eyes in case the strangers saw that he was awake.

"If it's going to be done, it's got to be done tonight," said the second voice. "I'm waking him up."

At this, a whole chorus of voices murmured their disapproval, but Jack was more worried about the strange sensation that something was climbing up the side of his bed. He could feel it tugging at his duvet: it was small, like a kitten. He could also hear the rattling of . . . belly beans. Then, before he could make up his mind what to do, something poked his face.

Terrified, Jack slapped the poking creature away. He heard a crunching noise as it hit the wardrobe. The deep, slow voice said, "Ouch," and the second voice said, "I've had just about enough of being hit!"

Jack groped for the switch on his lamp and turned it on. Blinking, he looked around his room. There was nobody there. The Christmas Pig was lying at the foot of the wardrobe.

Jack knew in his heart that he'd just hit the Christmas Pig. Even so, he wasn't ready to see the Christmas Pig get to his feet, put his trotters on his hips, and say, "If you hit me one more time, you horrible boy, I won't help you."

Jack was so shocked and scared he couldn't move. He remembered Mum once telling him that the way to find out whether you're dreaming is to pinch yourself. He tried it on his own leg. It hurt.

"You can talk!" whispered Jack.

"Clever, aren't you?" said the Christmas Pig, crossly.

"Jack *is* clever," said the croaky voice, which was coming from a battered old Matchbox car that had once belonged to Jack's dad. His hood was moving up and down as he talked, and his headlights had turned into eyes. "Stop being nasty to him. He's been through a lot of trouble you don't know about."

"I've been through trouble, too," said the Christmas Pig. "In case you've forgotten, he tried to pull my head off. And I'm offering to help him—on certain conditions, of course."

As if it wasn't strange enough to watch a cuddly pig and a toy car talking to each other, Jack now realized that lots of the other objects in the room had grown eyes and mouths, just like the car. The wardrobe had big brown eyes where there'd been knots of wood, and a mouth instead of a keyhole. His wastepaper basket had two little eyes on tin stalks, a bit like a snail's. Some of the Things had even sprouted arms: spindly metal ones on his bin, and floppy woolly ones on his rug. It was *sort of* exciting, but mostly terrifying.

"You've got to warn him how dangerous it will be," the Matchbox car was telling the Christmas Pig. "Otherwise he can't know what he's getting into."

There was a murmur of agreement from all the Things in the room.

"I didn't know," said Jack, finding his voice at last. "I didn't know Things could . . . talk."

CHAPTER 13

What he really meant to say was: I didn't know you could *feel*. He'd been very rough with these Things earlier and none more so than the Christmas Pig.

"We can only talk in the Land of the Living tonight, because it's a special night," said the Christmas Pig. "You know what night it is, don't you?"

"Christmas Eve," said Jack.

"Exactly," said the Christmas Pig. "And that means there's a chance—just for one night, we couldn't do it at any other time—that we can get your pig back."

"I know," said Jack, throwing back his duvet, which was one of the few things in the room that hadn't sprouted eyes and wasn't talking. "I'm going to the motorway."

"That won't work," said the Christmas Pig. "DP's in the Land of the Lost now and if you want to save him, you'll have to go and find him there and come home together."

"There's no such place as the Land of the Lost," said Jack scornfully. "You're making that up."

At that, most of the Things in his room began to talk at once: the box of tissues, both his slippers, and even the lampshade he'd brought to the new house from his old bedroom. It was extremely confusing and scary, and Jack didn't know whether he was more frightened of all these noisy Things waking up Gran and Grandpa, who'd stop him going outside to find DP, or of the Things themselves.

"I'll explain!" croaked the Matchbox car, and even though he was one of the smallest Things in the room, all the other Things fell silent, perhaps because he was one of the oldest. The car moved forward on his rusty wheels and spoke directly to Jack.

"The Land of the Lost is where Things go when you lose them," he said. "It's a strange and terrible place, governed by its own peculiar laws. I've been there many times, because you and your dad lost me so often."

"Sorry," said Jack nervously. It was true that he'd often forgotten where in the garden he had last played with the little car, which was why he was chipped and rusty.

"You always found me in the end," said the car, "and so, thank goodness, the Loser never got me."

"The who?" asked Jack.

"The Loser," the car repeated. "He rules the Land of the Lost. He's the reason Things fall out of pockets when you thought they were secure. He's the one who befuddles your mind so that you forget where you last put your pen. The Loser would like to suck every single Thing that belongs to humans down into his kingdom forever. He hates the living and he hates their Things, which he tortures and eats."

"The Loser's going to eat DP?" whispered Jack in terror.

"Not as long as DP abides by the laws of the Land of the Lost," said the car. "It's those who defy the law that the Loser's allowed to catch and eat. Unfortunately, the Loser makes the laws, and he sometimes cheats."

"I've got to rescue DP!" said Jack at once. "How do I get to this Land of the Lost?"

"You can't—or at least not alone," said the Christmas Pig.

"You're human, and it's a land of Things. That's how it usually works, anyway. But Christmas Eve is a night for miracles and lost causes. If you love DP enough to risk your life, then I'm ready to take you with me into the Land of the Lost, and we'll see whether we can bring him home again."

"I do love him enough," said Jack at once. "I love him enough for anything."

"All right, then," said the Christmas Pig. "I'll help you on one condition. After we've found DP and brought him home, I want you to return me to the girl who bought me."

"Why?" asked Jack.

"Because I like her," said the Christmas Pig. "*She* didn't stamp on me."

The old Matchbox car began to say something, but the Christmas Pig threw him a nasty look and the car fell silent.

"She won't take me back unless she knows you're happy with DP. So, do we have a deal?"

"Deal," said Jack at once. He didn't like the Christmas Pig, but knew that he needed him.

"You should put something on, instead of pajamas," said the Christmas Pig, "and take your slippers."

But Jack wasn't going to be bossed around by the new pig, and in any case, it felt too weird to put his feet in Things that were blinking at him, so he said, "I'm comfy as I am. Now take me to the Land of the Lost."

SHRUNK

The moment he spoke those words, Jack felt a strange sensation in the pit of his stomach. It was as though he was traveling downward, fast, in a lift. At the same time, the bed and the sheets beneath him began to grow so rapidly that he lost sight of the floor. In a panic, he tried to stand up, but he tripped over a wrinkle in the sheet and fell flat on his face.

Several seconds later, Jack realized that the bed hadn't grown at all. He'd shrunk. When he succeeded in standing up again, he saw that the creases in the sheets seemed like giant snowdrifts. It was very scary to think you could shrink like this, just by saying a few words, and Jack was very glad that his duvet didn't seem to have come alive, because it could have smothered him to death if it had wanted to.

The Christmas Pig's voice called up to him from the floor.

"Slide down the corner of the duvet!" he said. "Come on, it's quite easy!"

This wasn't true; however, Jack did his best, and after a frightening descent, which involved a big drop to the floor at the bottom, he finally landed beside the Christmas Pig. They were now exactly the same size: eight inches tall.

"Well, goodbye, everybody," said the Christmas Pig and he began to march toward Jack's bedroom door. "Nice meeting you."

Some of the Things in the bedroom tried to call them back.

"Think!" said a little plastic shark that Jack had bought at the Sea-Life Center, flapping its fins on the floor. "Think about what you're doing, Pig!"

"I have thought, thank you," said the Christmas Pig, leaning against the bottom of the door, which bounced open.

"No living child has ever entered the Land of the Lost!" wept a little robot Jack had once gotten free with a burger, and which he'd earlier thrown at the wall.

"There's a first time for everything," said the Christmas Pig as he and Jack walked out onto the landing.

"Jack, he's not telling you the—" began a pair of pants that had fallen out of one of Jack's drawers, but the Christmas Pig had placed his trotters beneath the door, where there was an inch of space, and tugged it shut again.

"Very boring Things you have," he told Jack. "Come on."

Thinking how rude the Christmas Pig was, and that he and Holly deserved each other, Jack followed the pig to the top of the stairs and copied him as he began lowering himself off each step onto the next. The bannisters were as tall as skyscrapers now that Jack was so small. They cast frightening shadows across the boy and the pig as they descended.

"Why aren't the stairs talking?" Jack asked, as he dropped from one to the next. "Why didn't my duvet?"

"Some Things aren't awake enough to talk, even on Christmas Eve," said the Christmas Pig. "Is your duvet new?"

"Yes," said Jack.

"Then it won't have had many of your feelings put into it yet. That's what wakes Things up. Being used and absorbing human feelings. Things like stairs and walls are taken for granted by humans, so they hardly ever get wakened."

"But *you're* new," said Jack. "And you're very awake."

A bit *too* awake, Jack thought privately, but he didn't say that out loud.

"I'm a special case," said the Christmas Pig and Jack thought this sounded boastful, and not at all the kind of comment DP would make, because DP never showed off.

"Now we need to decide where the best place to get lost is," said the Christmas Pig. "It's harder than you might think when you're trying to do it on purpose. Any ideas?"

"Is that all we have to do to get there?" asked Jack. "Get lost?"

"Of course, but it'll be hard, because I expect you know this house very well."

"It might be easier in the garden," said Jack. "Especially now I'm small. We could drag a chair to the back door, climb up to the lock, and open it."

"Good idea," said the Christmas Pig. They'd just reached the bottom of the stairs. "Which way?"

Jack led the Christmas Pig down the dark hallway toward the

kitchen. The hall seemed vast when you were only eight inches tall. One good thing was the big gap beneath the door into the kitchen. He and the Christmas Pig got down on their bellies and wriggled through.

"Excellent," said the Christmas Pig. "Now if we can just push the chair over to—"

But he never finished the sentence. A gigantic four-legged beast had risen up in front of them: a monster with long yellow teeth, shaggy fur, and gleaming eyes. With a deep bark, the monster launched itself at the Christmas Pig, skidding on the linoleum and almost catching the pig between its dangerous jaws.

"Run, run!" cried the Christmas Pig, sprinting back toward the door. Jack followed, Toby-the-dog's smelly breath hot on the back of his neck, his claws scrabbling on the floor. Together, Jack and the Christmas Pig threw themselves onto their tummies and dived back under the door, into the hall.

"You should have said there was a dog!" panted the Christmas Pig as he and Jack lay there, catching their breath.

"I forgot!" said Jack. "He doesn't usually live here!"

Toby-the-dog was whining and scratching on the kitchen side of the door, trying to reach them.

"It'll have to be the front door instead," said the Christmas Pig, picking himself up and dusting himself off. "Come on."

But at that moment, Toby-the-dog hurled himself against the kitchen door with such force that it burst open.

Jack and the Christmas Pig pelted back down the hall, Toby-the-dog slipping and sliding on the wooden floorboards behind

them. He chased them into the dark sitting room, so Jack and the pig dived under the sofa.

Toby-the-dog's shiny black nose appeared at the gap at the bottom, trying to snuffle them out. He whined loudly. Jack was afraid Toby-the-dog wouldn't give up while he knew they were under there.

"If we crawl behind the tree," Jack whispered to the Christmas Pig, "we could sneak back out of the room while he thinks we're still under here, and go to the kitchen door after all."

The Christmas Pig nodded. Holding his belly to keep his beans quiet, he followed Jack toward the gap at the other end of the sofa, where the Christmas tree stood. Its fairy lights were the only light in the room. Jack was now so small that the parcels beneath the tree loomed up in the darkness like higgledy-piggledy houses.

Toby-the-dog was still snuffling and pawing at the other end of the sofa. Slowly and cautiously, Jack crawled out and began to climb the presents. One of them was wrapped in scarlet ribbon, which was wonderful, because it gave somewhere for his bare feet to grip, but another, which was covered in blue paper patterned with silver snowflakes, tore a little as Jack grabbed it: a huge new box of LEGOs was inside, and Jack was sure that was from Dad. The twinkling lights above, which had seemed so tiny when he and Mum put them on the tree, now seemed huge and dazzled his eyes. Slowly he climbed toward the top of the mound of presents until he reached the biggest, which was wrapped in shiny gold paper. He'd be able to walk straight across this and then he'd be out from under the tree—but he slipped! The paper was so shiny Jack's feet slid on it, and unable to find anything to grab onto, he tumbled down a crevice, which was like a pitch-black ravine now that he was only eight inches tall. He tried to get out again, but he'd fallen between gigantic presents with smoothly wrapped sides.

"Where are you?" whispered the Christmas Pig, but a second later he, too, had slid down the slippery golden package and landed on top of Jack.

"Oh no!" said Jack, as they heard Toby-the-dog scampering toward the tree. "Why did you have to rattle?"

"Which way to the kitchen?" cried the Christmas Pig, as Toby-the-dog's growls grew ever louder.

"I don't know!" said Jack desperately. "I'm lost!"

Part Two
MISLAID

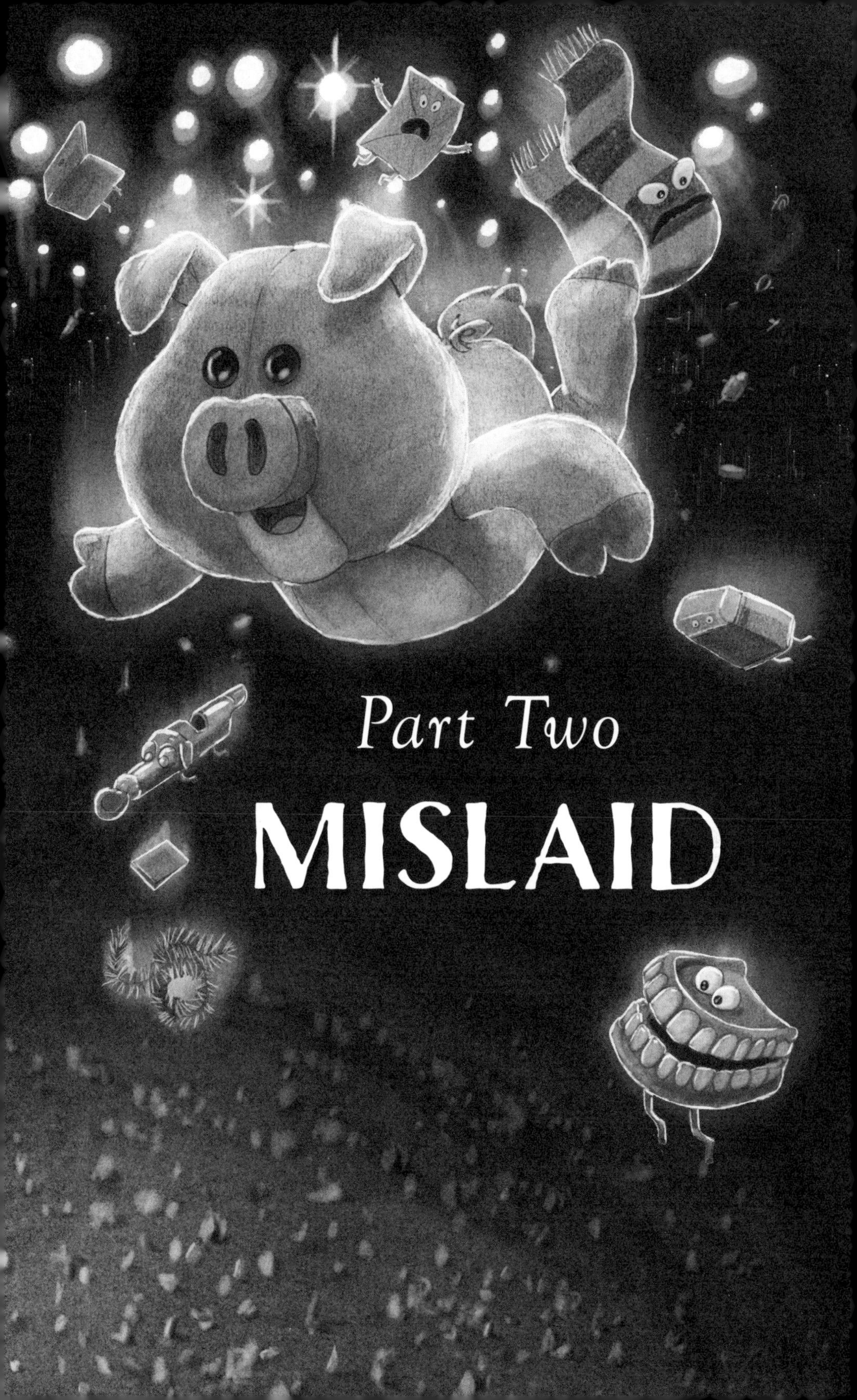

BENEATH THE TREE

With the word "lost," everything beneath Jack's feet vanished. He was falling—or rather, slowly sinking—down through the place where the floor should have been. It was as though he was trapped in some thick substance he couldn't feel or see. The tree lights had disappeared: all was inky blackness.

"Christmas Pig?" Jack called in panic.

"I'm here," came the Christmas Pig's voice out of the darkness. "Don't worry! This is how you enter the Land of the Lost! It'll be light in a moment!"

Sure enough, within a few seconds, Jack was able to see the Christmas Pig again. Like Jack, he was floating downward. Their surroundings became gradually lighter until Jack realized they were both sinking through their own column of golden light. Above them were two round holes in a wooden ceiling that Jack thought must be the floor of the world they'd left—*his* world, where Mum lived, where everything he knew existed.

Down, down, down they sank, and now Jack noticed that he and the Christmas Pig were far from the only Things sinking slowly through their columns of light. There were thousands upon thousands of them. Weightless, Jack was able to twist and turn, and in every direction he saw more sinking Things.

Nearest to Jack were a teaspoon, a shiny red Christmas bauble, a dog whistle, a pair of false teeth, a hand puppet, a shiny coin, a long string of tinsel, a camera, a screwdriver, a plane ticket, some sunglasses, a single sock, a teddy bear, and a roll of wrapping paper patterned with reindeer.

"You wouldn't think it was possible, would you?" the wrapping paper called to Jack. One of the reindeer on her surface was talking and blinking. "Third time she's lost me this evening! I've rolled under the radiator . . . She's panicking . . . Left the wrapping too late, as usual!"

The roll of paper had barely uttered these words when she reversed direction and began traveling up instead of down, toward the hole in the ceiling. As she rose out of sight, the wrapping paper shouted, "Yay, she's found me! Good luck! Hope you're back Up Top soon!"

Jack didn't answer, because he was too astonished by everything that was happening around him and, especially, what he could see of the floor below. At first, he thought he was looking down at a carpet of many different colors, but as he sank farther, he realized the carpet was really millions of Things. Scared, he scanned the floor for the Loser, but having no idea what the Loser looked like, he couldn't tell whether he was there or not. The lower Jack sank, the louder the noise: the Things on the floor were chattering and clattering and clinking and rustling, until the sound was almost deafening.

As their surroundings became lighter still, Jack realized that he was inside a gigantic building, like a warehouse, with immensely high brick walls and many holes peppering the wooden ceiling. The Things that had reached the ground, the rubber balls and diaries, the paper clips and tape measures, the cameras, pens, and purses, were all jabbering away in their groups. Jack was so fascinated by everything he was seeing that his landing took him by surprise. His bare feet touched the warm wooden floor, and the Christmas Pig landed beside him, in a pathway between a mass of jangling keys and an army of rustling umbrellas.

"We'll need a ticket," said the Christmas Pig briskly. "Come on."

The Christmas Pig led Jack off along the path between the keys on one side and the umbrellas on the other. They passed a knife, a skewer, and a long knitting needle. Jack could tell they were all important, because they each wore a peaked black hat with an "L" on it, which somehow stayed balanced on the tops of them even while they were hopping along. The Things in the hats were patrolling the edges of the path, making sure the others remained in their groups and keeping the walkway free for Things that had only just arrived.

"Those are the Loss Adjusters," the Christmas Pig muttered

to Jack. "I've heard about them from Things that have been here before. They're the Loser's servants. They enforce his laws in exchange for not being eaten."

A pair of long diamond earrings now landed in front of Jack and the Christmas Pig. They were sparkling so brightly Jack had to squint to look at them.

"Who's in charge here?" cried one of the earrings, in a grand voice.

"We're very valuable!" shouted her twin. "We require assistance!"

"Calm down, ladies," said a croaking tennis ball, bouncing up alongside Jack and the Christmas Pig. The ball looked as though it had been chewed by a dog, and was very smelly. "I've been through this a load of times before, I 'ave. It looks a mess, but they're organized."

The earrings seemed offended at being addressed by an object so filthy.

"I think we're in the wrong place!" cried the first earring, glittering as she turned on the spot, looking for assistance.

"Where do the *precious* Things go?" cried her sister.

But nobody answered. To their right, the keys kept yelling up at the distant holes in the ceiling, saying things like, "I'm in your other coat, you idiot!" or "You've left me in the lock again!" The umbrellas seemed quieter and sadder. Jack heard an old black one say, "I expect it's all over this time. He's left me on the train. He'll probably buy a new one . . ."

A tin opener in a black hat now approached, walking on metal legs. She had a small box around her neck and thin metal arms just below her handle.

"Tickets!" shouted the tin opener. "New arrivals, get your tickets here!"

"Let me do the talking," the Christmas Pig told Jack, but before he could ask for a ticket, the diamond earrings pushed in front of him.

"We're in the wrong place!" said the first earring.

"Where do *important* Things go?" asked the second.

"Jewelry's over there, by the west wall," said the tin opener, pointing. "But you need tickets first. Here—" She tore off two blue tickets from the little box hanging round her neck and gave one each to the earrings. "West wall," she repeated, because the earrings hadn't moved.

"I don't think you understand," said the first earring. "We're made of *real diamonds.*"

"You can't put us in with a bunch of common plastic beads," said the second earring. "Surely there's a place for valuables?"

"Get along to your waiting area," snapped the tin opener. "Diamonds or plastic, it's all the same down here. We'll soon know how much you're worth Up There."

Clearly offended, the earrings wiggled off toward the west wall.

The Loss Adjuster gave the tennis ball a blue ticket, too.

"Dog toys are over there, between shoes and schoolbooks."

It bounced away. The tin opener then turned to Jack and the Christmas Pig.

"Have you just arrived, too?"

CHAPTER 15

"Yes, we were lost together," said the Christmas Pig. "We fell out of our owner's pocket."

"Kids!" snorted the tin opener, tearing off two more blue tickets and handing them to Jack and the Christmas Pig. "They're responsible for half the Things down here, careless little brutes. When it's quiet, we can hear them crying from Up There. Ought to keep a tighter hold on Teddy if they don't want the Loser getting him, shouldn't they?"

"I suppose so," said the Christmas Pig.

"Nice workmanship," added the tin opener, looking at Jack. "Good detailing."

"Thank you," said Jack nervously.

"Children's toys are right over by the north wall," she added. You'll need a lift—it's too far to walk."

She gave a screeching whistle, and an old roller skate came zooming along the path toward them. It was the size of a golf cart compared to Jack and the Christmas Pig. They clambered inside, both just tall enough to see over the top.

The roller skate trundled off toward the place where the toys were waiting, and Jack felt a lurch of excitement: any moment now, he'd be seeing DP again!

MISLAID

They sped past lost playing cards, babies' shoes, lip balms, and pencil cases, and all the while, thousands upon thousands more lost Things floated down through golden shafts of light from the holes above.

As they neared the middle of the warehouse, Jack saw an enormous clock with four faces, positioned on a tall pillar so that every Thing could see it from wherever they were standing in the enormous building. At least, Jack thought it was a clock, but then he realized it had only one hand and no numbers. The colors of the rainbow ran around the outside of the face, and the clock's single hand was about to move out of yellow into green.

"I thought the Land of the Lost was supposed to be frightening," Jack said to the Christmas Pig.

The huge warehouse was certainly noisy and confusing, but Jack wasn't scared.

"We haven't gotten outside yet," said the Christmas Pig.

"But we don't need to go outside," said Jack. "You heard the tin opener. DP will be beside the north wall, with all the other toys."

"He won't," said the Christmas Pig. "He's been lost too long. I heard all about this bit from the keys of the shop where I was bought. They'd been here a lot. This place is called Mislaid. It's where Things go when they aren't properly lost yet. A human might just have put a Thing down for a couple of minutes, and forgotten where they left it, for example. Things are allowed to stay in Mislaid for one hour, to give them a chance of being found before they have to move out into the Loser's domain."

"DP's outside, where the Loser is?" Jack said, his excitement vanishing in an instant.

"Yes," said the Christmas Pig. "But don't worry. As long as he's obeying the law, he should be safe."

"But my Matchbox car said the Loser makes the laws, and he cheats!"

"That's true, he does," said the Christmas Pig, "but DP's a clever and sensible pig. I'm sure he won't do anything silly."

"How do *you* know DP's clever and sensible?" said Jack.

"Because we're brothers," said the Christmas Pig.

"But you've never met him!"

"That doesn't matter. He's my brother, and I'm his. We're the same."

"You aren't the same at all," said Jack, in case the Christmas Pig was about to suggest they go home, and Jack keep him, instead.

"No," said the Christmas Pig. "I forgot: there's something about me that makes you want to pull off my head."

"I told you I was sorry about that," said Jack.

"No, you didn't," said the Christmas Pig.

"All right, well I *am* sorry about it," said Jack.

After that, they didn't talk for a bit. The roller skate carried them past a great field of library books, their pages swishing as they discussed how they'd been lost.

"I think I can see toys!" said Jack at last.

Ahead of them, crowded into a huge area the size of five football fields, were dolls, plastic dinosaurs, model cars, skipping ropes, yo-yos, game cards, jigsaw pieces, and dominos: every kind of toy imaginable. Even though the Christmas Pig had told him DP wouldn't be there, Jack couldn't help hoping to see DP's wonky ears and button eyes, but there was no sign of him anywhere.

"What we need," said the Christmas Pig, as their roller skate slowed down, "is to find a pair of toys ready to swap tickets with us."

"Why?" asked Jack.

"Because then we'll be allowed out into the Land of the Lost without waiting an hour," explained the pig. "It should be easy. Everyone here wants to stay as long as they can, because the Loser can't touch them in Mislaid."

The roller skate came to a halt, they climbed out, and it scooted off again. Close by the place they were standing was a two-headed monster who was weeping into his hands. The monster was brown and lumpy, and a plastic princess in a pink dress and a tiara was comforting him.

"I can't believe he hasn't found me!" sobbed the monster. "And now I suppose he's fast asleep, dreaming of the new toys he'll get for Christmas, and I-I'll be eaten by the Loser!"

"Come on now, chins up," said the princess. "There's still time for him to find you."

"Ask those two to swap tickets," the Christmas Pig whispered to Jack, "but don't tell them why. They'll think it very strange that we're keen to leave Mislaid. Go on—you look like another action figure, so they'll trust you."

"What reason should I give for swapping?" asked Jack nervously.

The Christmas Pig thought hard, wrinkling up his snout.

"Tell the princess you think she's very pretty," he suggested, "and you'd like to protect her from the Loser and you're willing to swap tickets to keep her safe a bit longer."

Jack turned red.

"I'm not saying that!"

"I'll do it, then," said the Christmas Pig impatiently. He tugged Jack's ticket out of his hand and strode toward the princess and the two-headed monster, the beans in his belly rattling as he walked. "Princess," Jack heard the Christmas Pig saying, "my friend has noticed your friend's distress. Being a gallant young action fig—"

At that moment, a jack-in-the-box burst open unexpectedly, which caused a lot of toys nearby to scream with fright. Jack was glad of this, because it meant he couldn't hear all the embarrassing things the Christmas Pig was telling the plastic princess. Soon, the Christmas Pig was walking back toward him holding two green tickets instead of blue. Over the Christmas Pig's shoulder, Jack saw the two-headed monster blowing him kisses. He felt his face burning and turned away.

"The princess said she didn't need protecting and was quite

looking forward to an adventure," said the Christmas Pig, "but the monster made her swap with us. He wanted to kiss you, but I said you're too shy."

"Good," muttered Jack, taking his new ticket.

"We should be able to get out any moment now, with these tickets," said the Christmas Pig. "Aha!"

He pointed his trotter at the strange clock on the pillar. Its hand was moving from yellow to green. Now Jack realized that when the Timer's hand reached a new color, everybody who had a ticket of that shade had to leave Mislaid.

"Let's go," said the Christmas Pig, as a multitude of Things with green tickets began to move out of their enclosures and shuffle off toward the north wall. They all looked nervous.

The Christmas Pig squared his shoulders.

"This is where the real journey starts. Ready?"

"Ready," said Jack, nodding.

17 THE THREE DOORS

The thousands of green ticket holders formed untidy lines. There was much jostling and pushing. Many Things were still staring longingly up at the finding holes in the ceiling, hoping to be caught in a shaft of golden light and transported back up to the Land of the Living. Loss Adjusters in black hats pushed them onward with cruel laughs.

"Too late now—it's time for Allocation!"

"What does that mean?" Jack muttered to the Christmas Pig.

"I'm not sure," said the Christmas Pig, "but I think it must have to do with which part of the Land of the Lost we're sent to."

They joined a line behind a magnificent sapphire ring.

"*Would* you believe it," she was saying loudly to anybody who'd listen. "She took me off to wash her hands and *left me behind on the sink!*"

Jack looked anxiously toward the front of the line. At first, he couldn't see what lay there, but their line moved quickly and soon he realized that they were heading toward a long row of desks at which more Loss Adjusters sat, among them a mousetrap, a corkscrew, and a stapler. Beyond the desks were three gigantic doors: The first was made of plain wood, the kind you'd find on a barn or an outhouse. The second was made of shining steel, the sort you'd see on a safe or strong room. The last was made of shining gold and it was beautifully engraved with curling vines and flowers. Many of the Things in the lines were pointing at this third door with longing expressions.

One by one, the Things who'd reached the front of the lines were called forward to sit at one of the desks. The Loss Adjusters asked them questions, then, when the interview was over, the Loss Adjuster stamped their ticket and ordered them toward one of the doors.

"I'm worried," said the Christmas Pig suddenly.

"What about?" asked Jack.

"About how we're going to get you past the Loss Adjusters without them realizing you're human," said the Christmas Pig.

"The tin opener didn't realize," said Jack.

"But it wasn't her job to find out about you, or decide where you're sent next," said the Christmas Pig. "Quick, we need to come up with a story. What factory were you made in?"

"I . . . don't know," said Jack, trying but failing to think of a name that sounded like a factory's.

"Say the Dingledown Factory, Birmingham," said the Christmas Pig. "That was my factory and they made action figures as well as cuddly pigs. Now, what are you called?"

"Jack."

"Action figures aren't called Jack! We'll say . . . we'll say you're Pajama Boy, with the power of sleep and dreams."

"I don't want to be Pajama Boy," said Jack. "He sounds stupid."

"Then say you're called Jack and see what happens!" whispered the Christmas Pig fiercely as they moved ever closer to the front of the line. "Now, how were you lost?"

"I fell out of a boy's pocket," said Jack, copying what the Christmas Pig had said earlier to the tin opener.

"And where are you now?" asked the Christmas Pig.

"I'm here, talking to you," said Jack.

The Christmas Pig covered his face with his trotters. "We'll be lucky if we aren't thrown straight to the Loser." He removed his trotters again and said, "It's your Alivened bit that's been sucked down here into the Land of the Lost. You need to tell the Loss Adjuster where your plastic body is, see? Up in the Land of the Living!"

"This was your plan!" said Jack, frightened and a bit cross, because they were now close to the front of the line. "Tell me what I should say, quickly!"

But just then, an enormous commotion erupted behind them.

THE PRISONER

Two Loss Adjusters—a hole punch and a fork—were dragging a small and muddy Thing along between two lines, using the strong and spindly arms that so many Things seemed to grow in the Land of the Lost. Their prisoner was so filthy that it was almost impossible to see what he really was, although he seemed furry.

"Please!" the prisoner squeaked. "Please give me a ticket, let me stay for an hour! Oh, please, please, give me a chance! Somebody might want me . . . Oh, let me try—"

As the Loss Adjusters drew level with Jack and the Christmas Pig, Jack saw what the sobbing prisoner was: a tiny blue cuddly bunny who looked as though he'd lain in mud for days if not weeks. Jack couldn't understand why the Loss Adjusters were being such bullies to the poor bunny. The fork was poking him to force him along faster, and every time the bunny squealed in pain, the hole punch laughed, opening and shutting so that little circles of paper flew from her like confetti. They dragged their prisoner straight past two of the Loss Adjusters' desks and headed toward what looked like a metal manhole cover in the floor, which Jack hadn't noticed before.

"You belong to the Loser, you do!" said the hole punch. "Now stop making a scene in front of all these decent Things what have got owners Up Top!"

"Why are they treating him like that?" Jack whispered to the Christmas Pig, who merely shook his head, looking stricken.

"Is it because he's dirty?" Jack asked, thinking of grubby old DP. What if DP had been treated like that when he'd arrived in Mislaid?

"Never mind the bunny," said the Christmas Pig, suddenly looking determined. "This is your chance, Jack. Crawl."

"What?" said Jack.

"Crawl past the Loss Adjusters, quickly, while everyone's watching the bunny. I'll meet you on the other side!"

Now Jack understood: everybody was transfixed by the prisoner and his captors, even the Loss Adjusters at the desks. Jack sank to his knees, crawled past the sapphire ring and through the gap between two desks, toward a group of Things that had already been Allocated, and were standing in front of the wooden door. These Things were far too interested in the fate of the prisoner to notice Jack had joined them. Standing up, he turned to watch what was happening to the bunny now.

"Please!" he was squealing. "Oh, please, give me a chance—"

"There are no chances for Things like you," growled the fork as the bunny struggled. "Nobody wants you. Nobody cares you're lost. You're Surplus."

The hole punch dragged aside the heavy manhole cover, to reveal a dark hole. The bunny gave frightened squeaks as the fork prodded him closer and closer to the edge. At last, the little bunny slipped and fell. They heard his cry of terror growing fainter and fainter, as though he was sliding away down a chute, and then his scream was silenced by the hole punch slamming the metal lid back over the tunnel entrance.

The two Loss Adjusters straightened their black hats and hopped away, looking pleased with themselves. Slowly, all the Things who'd watched this horrible scene began to talk again.

A plastic comb standing beside Jack whispered, "Wasn't that dreadful?"

He had an odd appearance, having one eye on each side of him, and was speaking from a gap between his prongs.

"Yes," said Jack, "it was horrible."

He felt as though one of them should have tried to help the bunny instead of watching him get thrown down the chute. He wished he'd done something, but then he might have been recognized as a living boy and perhaps made to leave the Land of the Lost before he could find DP.

"It's disgusting, the way they treat Surplus," said a battery standing beside the comb, keeping her voice low in case a Loss Adjuster heard.

The Christmas Pig had now reached the front of the nearest line. The corkscrew Loss Adjuster, which had just sent the sapphire ring to wait beside the golden door, had a loud voice, so Jack was able to hear everything that passed between him and the pig.

CHAPTER 18

"Name?" asked the corkscrew.

"The Christmas Pig."

"Where were you made?"

"Dingledown Factory, Birmingham."

"Date and place of Alivening?"

"This afternoon," said the Christmas Pig, "in the Pendleton Toy Shop."

"And they've lost you already? Tut-tut," said the corkscrew. He examined a long list in front of him. "Christmas, Christmas, Christmas, Christmas . . . ah yes, here you are. Christmas Pig . . . Oh dear, nobody seems to like you very much, do they?"

"I'm a Replacement," said the Christmas Pig.

"Ah," said the corkscrew with a smirk, twisting in his chair. "Yes. Replacements sometimes work out and sometimes not. In your case, I see it's 'not.' But you're still brand-new, so if anyone finds you, they'll probably find a use for you. Charity shop, I expect. Wooden door."

So the Christmas Pig hurried to join Jack's group beside the wooden door, which now swung open.

HORSEY THINGS

An icy blast of air hit them as they walked outside. To Jack's surprise, because it had been night when he'd left the Land of the Living, the sun was only just setting outside the warehouse. Snow was falling from a strange sky, which looked as though it was made of painted wood, though it was far, far higher than any ceiling in the Land of the Living. Jack could see a few distant finding holes in the wooden sky, but not nearly as many as there'd been in the ceiling of Mislaid.

The land all around them was bleak and empty: a stony wasteland, which stretched away into the distance, with only clumps of thistles growing there. Between the barren ground and the swirling snow, it was the most unwelcoming place Jack had ever seen.

He glanced over his shoulder at the wall of Mislaid and saw to his amazement that the door they'd just come through had vanished. And then it struck him that there was no way back now, unless he found DP. He was starting to fear that the Land of the Lost was even stranger and more complicated than he'd first thought. For instance, what would the Things who'd gone through the other doors see when they got to the other side? And most importantly: which door had DP gone through?

Then Jack heard the sound of hooves. He and the rest of the group—who apart from the comb and the battery included a little plastic ruler, an eraser in the shape of a panda, some shoelaces, and a pair of chopsticks—turned to see a number of horse-shaped Things approaching. There were plastic ponies, a cuddly pink unicorn, a pottery cart horse, and largest of the lot, a big wicker donkey carrying baskets of plastic fruit on either side of its saddle. At the head of all these different Things rode another Loss Adjuster: a pair of kitchen scissors wearing two black hats, one for each of his handles. He was mounted, ends downward, on a wooden horse with squeaky wheels.

"Hurry up, get on!" snapped the scissors. "No!" he added sharply to Jack and the Christmas Pig, who were headed toward two of the plastic ponies. "You're the biggest. You can share the donkey."

So Jack and the Christmas Pig clambered onto the donkey, which gave a groan and said, "Mind my wicker. It *can* snap, you know."

Most of the other Things had great difficulty mounting their horses. The comb, the battery, the ruler, and the chopsticks kept sliding off, and the scissors ended up instructing the shoelaces to tie them on.

Just as everybody had successfully mounted, a wailing Klaxon sounded from behind the wall of Mislaid.

"Oh dear," said Scissors, startled. "That's not good."

"What does it mean?" asked the comb, sounding panicked.

"It means," said Scissors, "that some Thing is where it shouldn't be."

Jack and the Christmas Pig exchanged worried looks. Jack was sure the Christmas Pig was thinking the same as him: somehow, the Loss Adjusters knew Jack was there, even though he'd avoided questioning.

"Will the Loser come?" whispered the ruler, who was trembling.

"Maybe," said the scissors. "If a Thing's disobeyed the rules, the Loser'll want to catch 'em and eat 'em. You disobey the rules, you become Surplus, and Surplus gets eaten, always has, always will. That's the law."

Scissors cast a sharp look over the group of Things on their horses. "You've all been Allocated right and proper, haven't you?" he asked.

They all nodded and said yes.

Scissors kicked his wooden horse on. Its squeaky wheels began to turn, and all of them set off along a snowy trail that led around the outskirts of the wasteland.

"Well, if you're lying, we'll find out soon enough," said Scissors in a grim voice.

THE WICKER DONKEY

"Why is it still daytime?" Jack whispered to the Christmas Pig as they set off, the wicker donkey creaking as it walked. "It was dark when we left my bedroom."

"Time's different in the Land of the Lost," the Christmas Pig whispered back. "They say an hour in the Land of the Living is a whole day in the Land of the Lost."

The snow fell thickly and soon the shoulders of Jack's pajamas were cold and wet, although that didn't worry him nearly as much as the possibility that the Loser was about to loom out of the darkness. However, nothing happened except that the battery slipped a little on her plastic pony, and the shoelaces binding her on had to tighten themselves.

Even though the sky had that oddly painted appearance, it slowly darkened as they rode around the edge of the wasteland.

Soon, night had fallen. Jack only knew that Scissors was still leading them because he could hear the squeak of his horse's wheels. Jack whispered to the Christmas Pig, "Where d'you think they're taking us?"

"I don't know," said the Christmas Pig, "but we'll obey orders for now. All the Things I've ever known have told me that breaking the Loser's laws is the quickest way to get eaten. He lives out there," the Christmas Pig added, pointing one of his trotters at the wide stony wasteland. "That's the Wastes of the Unlamented."

"What does 'Unlamented' mean?" asked Jack.

"It means no human cares you've gone," said the Christmas Pig, staring out over the bleak landscape. "It's where Surplus goes—Things that are unloved and unwanted and useless. They don't get any shelter. They just roam around on the Wastes, until the Loser catches them."

"Well, DP *definitely* can't be on the Wastes," said Jack. "He's more loved and wanted than anything down here, I expect."

"No, he can't be out there," agreed the Christmas Pig, looking away from the Wastes at the dirt track ahead. "If we're lucky, he'll be wherever we're going. It must be a place for cheap Things, by the looks of this group."

"DP isn't cheap," said Jack at once. "He's very valuable."

"He's valuable to *you*, but we pigs aren't expensive," said the Christmas Pig. "I only hope nobody thinks it's strange when his identical twin turns up."

"Oh, don't worry about that," said Jack. "You don't look anything like DP. He's a different color. His eyes have fallen out and he's got buttons instead. His ears are wonky and he smells better."

Their wicker donkey creaked and swayed. The battery whimpered as she slid sideways off her pony yet again, and the shoelaces gripped her even more tightly.

"What d'you mean, he smells better?" asked the Christmas Pig.

"I don't know—he smells like DP, that's all."

"And how do I smell?" asked the Christmas Pig.

"Of toy shop and carpet," said Jack. "It's a nothing-smell."

"Thanks very much," said the Christmas Pig.

After that there was silence except for the clip-clop of pottery and plastic hooves, the creaking of the wicker donkey, and the squeaking of the wheels on Scissors's horse. At last, Scissors shouted, "Welcome home!"

Out of the darkness loomed a battered wooden sign on which was written in flaky paint: WELCOME TO DISPOSABLE.

Part Three

DISPOSABLE

DISPOSABLE

"Oh no—oh no—the shame of it!" cried Comb. "We're disposable!"

"Not complaining, are you?" said Scissors in a menacing voice. "Because at least you're getting a roof over your head. There's plenty that don't. If you'd rather be Surplus, it could be arranged!"

"No," whispered Comb, terrified, "I wouldn't rather be Surplus."

"Stop your whining, then," snapped Scissors.

The town they'd just entered was comprised of low wooden buildings, all of which looked drafty and flimsy. A few feeble lanterns lit the snowy street. Scissors led the group to a hitching post, where he dismounted, tied up all their mounts, and set the battery, the comb, the ruler, and the chopsticks free.

"Howdy!" said a cheery voice behind them, and everybody turned around to see a pair of spectacles bouncing out of a building with swing doors that was labeled SALOON. Spectacles was wearing a black Stetson with an "L" on it, and looked far friendlier than any Loss Adjuster they'd met so far.

"Good to see you, friends!" he cried, beaming, his nose pads flapping like a big mustache. "I'm Sheriff Specs! Say, Scissors: we heard a rumor that the Klaxon went off in Mislaid an hour ago. Is it true?"

"It's true, all right," said Scissors. "Some Thing's where it shouldn't be."

"Bless my hinges, that'll mean trouble!" said Specs anxiously. He pulled a ragged duster out of thin air, wiped his lenses, then made it magically disappear again while peering more closely at the group. "All righty, I'll take these folks inside and give 'em the introduction. Have a shot of lubricant before you head off, Scissors?"

"No time," said Scissors.

"But you might freeze up, riding back in these conditions."

"Hmm . . . you've got a point," said Scissors, now looking toward the saloon.

"And you've got two!" said the sheriff, roaring heartily at his own joke. "Get it? Get it?"

He looked hopefully around at the group. Nobody laughed. Comb sniffed.

"Follow me, then, folks!" said Specs, and he led the way into the saloon. Scissors followed, right behind Jack. It made the back of Jack's neck prickle to hear his sharp points hitting the ground.

The bar was lit by a single flickering oil lamp. Moth-eaten velvet curtains hung at the windows, and the wooden floorboards were stained. An old gardening glove was playing a mournful tune on a toy piano in the corner. In the ceiling was another finding hole, and right below it, taking up two seats, was an old tin lunch box.

"That there's Fingers, at the piano," said Specs, and Fingers the glove waved her thumb and went back to playing her sad tune, "and that there's Lunchy, sitting 'neath the finding hole."

The lunch box didn't say anything, but kept staring up at the dark hole in the ceiling, as though she could will a beam of golden light to appear and take her back to the Land of the Living. Jack couldn't blame her for wanting to leave this gloomy room. He looked around to see whether DP was sitting in one of the shadowy corners, but he wasn't there. Perhaps, Jack thought, he was asleep in one of the ramshackle houses they'd passed outside. He was wondering how soon he'd be able to sneak out to look, when Specs said, "All righty, then, why don't we all draw up a chair and get cozy?"

They all sat down. The draft coming through the swing doors was icy cold and Jack was now doing his best not to shiver. He wished he'd done what the Christmas Pig had suggested back in his bedroom, and brought a hoodie and some shoes, although he wasn't going to tell the pig that.

"So, welcome to Disposable!" said the sheriff. "We ain't got much in this town, but what we've got, we share! Now, I understand"—he glanced at the sniffing comb—"some of you ain't too happy to be here—"

"How could *any* Thing be happy to find themselves in Disposable!" said Comb, breaking into sobs. "It means our owners don't care about us!"

CHAPTER 21

The chopsticks drooped a little at that—Things in the Land of the Lost seemed to become extra bendy, quite apart from having mouths and eyes and arms—and the panda eraser sighed.

"Now, that's not true, sir!" said Specs firmly. "If nobody cared about you, you'd have been shoved down the Waste Chute in Mislaid!"

"I th-thought I was special to him!" sobbed Comb, ignoring Specs and pulling a single black hair out from between his teeth. "We've been together for y-years . . . I thought h-he cared!"

"Come on now, friend, buck up," said the sheriff gently. "We cheap, old Things know how it is. Nobody's heart broke when we disappeared. We're easy to replace. But that doesn't make us worthless, no sirree!" continued Specs. "There's still hope—lots of it! Why, any of you might be found at any moment!"

"I've never even been used," said Battery, looking glum. "You'd think I'd be worth more to the family than this. It's Christmas, after all. I thought I'd have a job for life inside the little girl's new remote-controlled car."

"Well, now you know, Battery!" wailed Comb. "You're worthless to them! We're *all* worthless!"

"What you need is a good night's sleep, sir!" said the sheriff, getting back onto his arms and inviting Comb to stand up, too. "Everything will seem better after you've rested. You hurry along to room number sixteen, now. Up the stairs, first on the right. Off you go, there's a good fellow."

Comb looked as though he'd like to argue, but at that moment, a horrible scream echoed down the street outside. Fingers, the gardening glove, stopped playing the piano. Specs, Scissors, and even Lunchy turned sharply in the direction of the Wastes.

"What was that?" squealed Comb.

"What happens on the Wastes is best ignored," said Scissors, who was now drinking his glass of lubricant beside the bar. "Just do as you're told and if you're lucky, you'll never find out what causes the screams."

ADJUSTMENTS

Once Comb had disappeared upstairs, Specs said, "Why don't Fingers play us some Christmas carols, brighten things up?"

The gardening glove began to play "O Little Town of Bethlehem" but it didn't really help. Jack could tell all the Things were still thinking—as he was—of the scream.

"Now," Specs said to the remaining newcomers, "the rules here are simple. Just stay within the town limits—and keep cheerful! Never forget, at any minute you might be found—or Adjusted!"

"Adjusted?" repeated the Battery. "What does that mean?"

"It means your value Up There has changed," said the sheriff. "Take your case, Battery. Nobody thinks they need you right now. But let's say they pull off the back of the little girl's remote-controlled car on Christmas Day and realize they haven't got enough batteries without you! That's when you become much more important to them. They'll start looking for you harder, and while they're looking, you'll be moved to Bother-It's-Gone—that's the next town—because you've become that much more important to your owners. In Bother-It's-Gone, you get your own little house, maybe even with a garden! But if you end up staying in Disposable forever, folks, then I hope you'll help me make this the happiest, most vibrant town in the Land of the Lost!"

Jack now felt certain DP must be in Bother-It's-Gone. They needed to get out of Disposable as quickly as possible and head there instead.

"All righty, let's get you all bedded down for the night," said Specs. "I'm afraid some of you will need to share a room, because we're a little cramped in Disposable—"

"Nobody's as cramped as me!" said a wheezy, echoing voice. Everyone looked around to see who'd spoken, but there wasn't anyone else in the bar.

"That you, Haley?" said Specs, grinning in the direction of the lunch box, who looked very embarrassed.

"Yes!" said the wheezy voice, which Jack now realized was coming from inside the tin box. "Can't I come out for a bit? *Please?* It's so dark in here, and it smells of egg sandwich!"

"No!" snapped Scissors from the bar. "You stay put! Things that are lost inside Things that are lost must stay lost in the Things that were lost. That's the law!"

Jack looked at the Christmas Pig, but he didn't seem to have understood this any more than Jack had.

"But it's horrible in here!" wailed the voice.

"It won't be forever!" the lunch box told her tummy.

"Ha!" said Scissors, with a cruel smile. "Don't kid yourself.

There's probably a nice new lunch box waiting under the Christmas tree for your owner right now. Pink, with unicorns on the lid, I 'spect. You think she'll bother looking for an old tin like you, once she's got something nice and new and plastic?"

With a sob, Lunch Box jumped off the two chairs and clattered away up the stairs toward the bedrooms, while the wheezy voice inside her said, "Ouch! *Ouch!* You're shaking me around!"

"That warn't kind, Scissors," said Specs in a low voice.

"Kind?" spat Scissors. "It's the truth. Things need to know their place. That's how we all stay out of trouble."

He poured the last drops of lubricant over the screw holding him together, then stalked out of the bar on his sharp points, into the swirling snow.

Specs sighed, then told each new Thing which number room they were to sleep in. One by one the Things headed up the stairs, until only Jack and the Christmas Pig were left.

Now Specs seemed to notice them for the first time.

"We don't usually get things as new as you in Disposable," he said, looking curiously at the Christmas Pig. "What's your story, Pig?"

"Oh, we were lost together," said the Christmas Pig. "We both fell out of our boy's pocket."

"What kind of boy wouldn't look for two fine toys like yourselves?" asked the sheriff, peering from the Christmas Pig to Jack. "What are you, anyway?" he asked, staring into Jack's face.

"I'm an action figure," said Jack. "Pajama Boy, with the power of sleep and dreams. I've got my own cartoon," he added, to make himself more important.

"Your own cartoon, you say?" said Specs, still gazing at Jack. "Well, well. Remarkable detailing. So you both fell out of your owner's pocket?"

"Our owner's a very spoiled boy," said the Christmas Pig. "He doesn't care about his toys, because he's got so many. As far as he's concerned, one stuffed pig is very much like another stuffed pig, one action figure much like the next. He's even been known to throw his Things around and stamp on them," the Christmas Pig added, with half a glance at Jack, who scowled.

"Dearie me, I've heard there are such children," said Specs sadly. "Back in my day, children had fewer toys and treasured them. We'd never have seen such fine specimens as yourselves here in olden times.

"Let me walk you up to your room," Specs went on. "You won't mind sharing, since you know each other already?"

He led them upstairs, and then along a dark, windowless upstairs corridor with numbered doors on either side. As they passed number twenty-three, the door opened a crack and the tin lunch box peered out.

"Am I being Adjusted?" she whispered.

"Don't look like it, Lunchy," said Specs. "We normally hear about Adjustments earlier in the day than this."

The lunch box sighed and closed her door again.

"Poor Thing," said Specs quietly as they walked on down the corridor. "Finding it hard to settle in."

"Sheriff Specs," said Jack suddenly—he had to make absolutely sure that DP wasn't here, so he ignored the warning look the

Christmas Pig was giving him—"have you seen another toy pig here in Disposable? He's around the same height as this pig, but he's got buttons for eyes and his ears are lopsided."

"A pig with button eyes and lopsided ears?" said Specs, pausing in the darkness to peer at Jack again. "No, son, I can't say I've seen any pig matching that description."

Jack was disappointed but not really surprised. Specs pushed open the creaking door of bedroom twenty.

"Sleep well, fellas," he said.

But he gave Jack a very suspicious look as he closed the door behind him.

THE PLAN

The moment Specs had gone, the Christmas Pig rounded on Jack. "What did you ask him about DP for?"

"Because that's why we're here—to find him!" said Jack.

"Isn't it obvious he can't be in Disposable? Why would you draw attention to us like that? And what was all that about having your own cartoon?" the Christmas Pig added angrily.

"Well, Pajama Boy's a stupid name," said Jack, just as crossly, "and there has to be a reason a factory made an action figure. Why would anyone make a plastic boy in pajamas?"

"I only hope Specs doesn't tip off the Loser that there's an action figure around here who's acting a lot like a living boy who's lost a cuddly pig!" said the Christmas Pig. "If the Loss Adjusters start asking other toys whether they've ever heard of Pajama Boy and his cartoon, we're really going to be in trouble. We mustn't do *anything else* to draw suspicion to ourselves while we're thinking up a plan."

As Jack couldn't think of a good retort to this, he sat down on the double bed, which made the mattress springs creak, and looked around. The room was lit by a single candle, and the wallpaper was peeling. Cobwebs stretched across the finding hole in the ceiling. Clearly, nobody had been found in this room for a very long time. Meanwhile, the Christmas Pig had moved to the cracked window, and was staring down into the snowy street.

Jack was far too worried about DP to sleep, so after a while, he got up and joined the Christmas Pig at the window. Snow was still falling thickly into the dark street outside. Scissors and the horses were gone.

"Christmas Pig?" said Jack, after a long stretch of silence.

"Hm?" said the Christmas Pig.

"What does 'Alivening' mean? Is it like the waking up you told me about?"

"That's it," said the Christmas Pig, still looking down into the dark snowy street.

"And it happens when human feelings rub off on Things?"

"It's not really rubbing off," said the Christmas Pig. "The feelings come *inside* us. Alivening is what changes us from fabric and beans and fluff, or metal and wood and plastic, into . . . something more. It can take a Thing years to be fully Alivened—but sometimes it comes all at once. That's the way it happened to me, today, in the toy shop. Holly and your grandpa were discussing which pig to take home to you, and when they chose me, I was Alivened. That's when I began to mean something. The Alivening is when we truly understand what we were made to do."

"Is that why you want to belong to Holly?" asked Jack. "Because she chose you?"

"Yes," said the Christmas Pig, after a little hesitation. "That's wh—"

But just then, noises in the street below made them both peer back out of the window.

"Someone's coming!" said Jack, scared. He could see more black hats at the end of the street. Were they coming to find the Thing that shouldn't be here?

Three new Loss Adjusters—a razor, a chisel, and a penknife—were coming down the street, each of them driving a funny-looking sledge or carriage: an old slipper pulled by a clockwork mouse, a shoebox dragged by a fuzzy toy dog, and a wooden cart with wheels, which was being pulled along by two elephant ornaments, one made of marble and one of brass. Three passengers—a bus pass, a key, and a passport—sat in each of the vehicles, behind the Loss Adjuster who was driving. As Jack and the Christmas Pig watched, the carriages stopped beneath the lantern outside the saloon, and Sheriff Specs came bustling out onto the street to greet them.

Slowly and carefully, the Christmas Pig opened the window. It gave a little squeak, but fortunately, the new arrivals were making too much noise down below to hear it, and now Jack and the Christmas Pig were able to hear what Specs and the Loss Adjusters were saying.

"Howdy, friends!" cried Specs. "I was expecting you an hour ago!"

"We got held up—there's a new checkpoint," said the penknife, who wore a furry black hat. "Haven't you heard? Seems there's a Thing down here that *shouldn't be in the Land of the Lost at all.*"

CHAPTER 23

"Shiver my screws, you don't say?" gasped Specs. "When's the last time *that* happened?"

"I can't recall it *ever* happening," said Penknife. "You seen any Thing acting oddly, Specs?"

"Well, now," said Specs slowly. "Funny you should say that . . . I was just talking to a pair of toys who I thought was acting a mite oddly."

Jack and the Christmas Pig exchanged frightened glances.

"Then you'd better contact Captures, at once," said Penknife sternly. "The Loser'll eat you as well as them, if it turns out they're the Things that shouldn't be here. Anyway—here you are. Three new citizens for Disposable, from Bother-It's-Gone. Oy, you three!" he shouted rudely at the passengers sitting in the vehicles. "Out!"

"Now, now," said Specs as the bus pass, key, and passport all climbed down into the street, where they stood huddled together, looking miserable. "There's no need to treat 'em rough, just because they've been Adjusted."

"I'm in a hurry," snapped Penknife. "It's the usual story for these three. They've all been replaced Up There, so the trouble they caused is over. But I've got an order to Adjust three of yours. Here—" He handed Specs his list.

"Pokey," Specs read out loud. "Hm, I had a hunch she wouldn't be with us long. Fingers—oh dear," said Specs sadly, "we'll miss her at the piano. And—bless my nose pads—Lunchy, too?"

"The mum's realized her little girl's lost inhaler is inside her," said Penknife. "The girl's got asthma. The mum's keen to find that lunch box, now."

Jack suddenly gripped the Christmas Pig's soft arm.

"What?" whispered the pig.

"We could hide inside Lunch Box, and go to the next town!"

"What if they make Lunch Box open, at the checkpoint?" said the Christmas Pig.

"I—I don't know," Jack admitted, frightened at the prospect, "but what if Specs reports us to Captures?"

The Christmas Pig thought for a few seconds, his snout crinkled up, then said, "All right—but leave the talking to me, and *don't* mention having a cartoon! Take the blanket off that bed," he added, "it's cold out there. I told you, you should have put on something warmer."

"I'm fine," snapped Jack, but when the Christmas Pig had turned his back, Jack sneaked the blanket off the bed and followed.

LUNCH BOX

Jack and the Christmas Pig crept out of their room and back along the dark corridor, the pig holding his belly tight to muffle the sound of his beans, until they reached door number twenty-three. Jack knocked softly, and the old tin lunch box opened it.

"D'you mind if we come in?" asked the Christmas Pig.

"Not at all," Lunch Box said politely, though she sounded surprised.

Lunch Box's room was quite as dark and shabby as the one they'd left, and even smaller. It looked over the back of the saloon, across the many low wooden houses of Disposable. Snow was still falling heavily past the window.

"Good news!" the Christmas Pig told Lunch Box. "The Adjusters have just arrived. If you can prove you've got an inhaler inside you, they're going to take you out of Disposable!"

"Well, of course I can prove it!" cried Lunch Box joyfully and she let her lid fall open. Sure enough, inside sat a glum-looking inhaler, who said in a wheezy voice, "If *I'm* the reason we're being Adjusted, why can't I—"

But she didn't finish her question, because the Christmas Pig had just jumped into the lunch box beside her and covered her mouth with his trotters. Jack squeezed inside, too. It was very cramped, and he could smell the egg sandwiches.

"That's *extremely* rude!" said Lunch Box's shocked voice from above them. "You can't just walk in without an invitation!"

"Shut your lid!" said the Christmas Pig fiercely. "Or we'll tell them you offered to smuggle us to the next town, and you'll be chucked out onto the Wastes for helping Surplus!"

"Get out! Get out!" cried the lunch box, jumping up and down as she tried to dislodge them, but Jack and the Christmas Pig clung on. "I'll tell them you jumped in and tried to *make* me smuggle you!"

"It'll be our word against yours!" said the Christmas Pig. "And what's more, if you don't help us, my action figure friend here will break this inhaler, and if the inhaler's broken, you'll *never* be Adjusted! Pajama Boy's got remarkably fine fingers, you know! Perfect for breaking Things!"

Even though the whole idea of getting inside the lunch box had been Jack's, he now felt both frightened and guilty. He couldn't help feeling sorry for the lunch box and he *definitely* didn't want to break the inhaler. He was also shocked at how mean the Christmas Pig was being to these poor Things, but before he could say any of this, there was a knock on the door.

"Lunchy?" came old Specs's voice from outside in the corridor.

CHAPTER 24

At once, Lunch Box slammed her lid shut, leaving Jack and the pig squashed together in the dark with the inhaler.

"Yes?" they heard Lunch Box say in a quavering voice.

"Good news. You're being Adjusted!"

"Oh," came Lunch Box's muffled voice. "Um . . . wonderful."

"You all right, dearie? You don't sound that pleased."

"No, I . . . I am. I'll just—I'll just miss you, Specs."

"Well, now," said the sheriff, sounding touched. "Ain't that sweet! But you'd better hurry! The Adjustment Team's running late!"

The lunch box's lid was a little bit warped, which was lucky as it let in enough air for Jack to breathe, not to mention a tiny ray of light. Squashed together inside the dark tin, Jack and the Christmas Pig felt the lunch box hopping downstairs into the bar.

Lunchy's tin bottom made such a racket crossing the wooden floor that Jack felt safe to whisper to the Christmas Pig, who still had his trotters clamped over the inhaler's mouth, "There was no need to threaten her like that!"

"D'you want to find DP, or not?"

"Of course I do," said Jack, "but you were horrible!"

"Says the boy who tried to pull off my head," said the Christmas Pig.

"Stop going on about that! I've *said* I'm sorry!"

The lunch box kept bouncing along, and Jack knew they'd reached the street when they heard the penknife's voice, quite close by. "You there, Lunch Box—you ride in my wagon, as you're biggest. Here, Chisel—help her up."

"No, no, I can manage!" said Lunch Box, sounding scared. Jack guessed she didn't want any of the Loss Adjusters to feel how heavy she was, when she was only supposed to have an inhaler inside her. She made several little jumps, then finally managed to land with a clunk inside the wooden wagon.

"Sorry I'm late!" came a new voice. "I'm *so* pleased to be going! Not that you haven't been kind, Specs—*very* kind—but I won't miss sharing a room with Hanky. He hasn't washed since he got here."

"Poor fella," said the sheriff sadly. "He's given up. Some Things do, when they haven't been found for years. Well, good luck, Pokey! Goodbye, Fingers! Goodbye, Lunchy! We'll miss you!"

"So long, Specs," called Penknife. "Mind you contact Captures about those toys, now!"

The wooden wagon moved off. Jack could hear the footsteps of the two heavy elephants crunching in the snow, the buzz of the clockwork mouse, and the occasional yap of the fuzzy dog.

"I'm going to let go of you now," the Christmas Pig whispered to the inhaler. "But if you scream or give us away, we'll make sure you get thrown onto the Wastes with us!"

The inhaler gave a little puff, which seemed to be her way of agreeing, and the Christmas Pig let her go. She drew a long wheezy breath, then whispered, "You're both very rude and nasty, but it's also nice to see something apart from the inside of this tin, so hello and welcome."

The three carriages moved on for what felt like at least an hour, and Jack was getting quite tired of the smell of egg sandwiches, when they heard a voice from up ahead.

CHAPTER 24

"HALT!"

The wooden wagon trundled to a stop. Jack and the Christmas Pig looked at each other and Jack could tell from the expression in the pig's little black plastic eyes that he, too, was scared.

"Documents!" said a rasping voice.

They heard the shuffling of papers.

"One Pokémon card, Pokey, owner's realized could be valuable—check," said the cruel voice. "One gardening glove, Fingers, owner can't find new ones as comfortable—check. One lunch box, Lunchy, owner's remembered there's an inhaler inside her."

Something banged hard on the side of Lunch Box, who let out a yelp of pain.

"You in there, Inhaler?" snarled the voice.

"Yes!" called the inhaler.

"*Check,*" said the cruel voice. "All right, you can proceed. Keep your eyes peeled, though, Penknife. We're on high alert. I s'pose you've heard there's some Thing down here that shouldn't be?"

"Yes. Any description yet?" asked Penknife.

"Not yet," said the cruel voice. "But I've never seen the Loser so angry."

"You've seen him?" said Penknife nervously.

"Oh yes," said the cruel voice. "He told me, 'The night for miracles and lost causes won't last forever. Once it's over, finders keepers.'"

"What does that mean?" asked Penknife.

"No idea," snarled the cruel voice. "Just keep watch for any Thing acting strangely!"

With that, the wooden cart rolled on again.

"He *dented* me," Lunchy complained to Penknife.

"Well, that's Hammer for you," said Penknife. "Never looks when he can bash!" He raised his voice to address all three passengers. "You lot might as well get comfy and sleep, if you can. We've got a long way to go."

The cart now started to move uphill. Jack, who found himself forced to the back of the lunch box, managed to curl up in a corner, wrapped in the blanket he'd brought from Disposable, with his face lying against the Christmas Pig's soft head. It wasn't at all like curling up with DP, but it was comfier than leaning against the cold tin wall.

Part Four

BOTHER-IT'S-GONE

BOTHER-IT'S-GONE

Jack jerked awake. Something soft was prodding him, and after a moment, he realized it was the Christmas Pig's trotter again. The cart was still moving. A ray of bright light was falling through the dent in Lunchy's lid. Inhaler was still fast asleep, making little wheezy noises.

"Time to get out!" the Christmas Pig whispered in Jack's ear. "Penknife's just said we're nearly at Bother-It's-Gone! We'll slip out of Lunchy, then jump off the back of the cart."

"What if we're spotted?"

"Well, then, we'll just have to run as fast as we can. Ready?"

"All right," whispered Jack, suddenly very scared.

"Lunchy?" said the Christmas Pig, prodding her side. "Are you awake?"

"Yes," she whispered back.

"Let us out, please, and don't forget: if you tell anyone you saw us, we'll tell them you helped us!"

CHAPTER 25

Lunchy's lid clicked open. Clutching his belly to stop the sound of his beans giving them away, the Christmas Pig climbed out of the lunch box into the bright sunshine and Jack followed, leaving Inhaler snoozing behind them.

Luckily, the wooden cart was last in the line of vehicles, and as Penknife, who was driving, had his back to them, nobody saw Jack and the Christmas Pig emerge from the tin.

"I know you didn't want to help, but thanks all the same, Lunchy!" the Christmas Pig whispered, and he patted her gently on the lid.

"You were very rude," the lunch box whispered back, "but I hope the Loser doesn't get you. Good luck!"

Slowly and carefully, Jack and the Christmas Pig climbed over the back of the wooden cart, let themselves fall into the soft snow, then darted out of sight behind a clump of fir trees beside the trail.

Looking around, Jack saw that the cart had taken them to the top of a mountain, from which they could look down on the wide stretches of the Wastes of the Unlamented. Disposable was no longer visible, nor could Jack see anything moving on the Wastes. He supposed the Loser had eaten all the latest arrivals, unless the poor Things were hiding in clumps of thistles.

Turning to watch the three carriages, he saw them disappear into the town, which was perched on the very top of the mountain. A glossy painted sign near Jack and the Christmas Pig's hiding place gleamed in the sunlight. On it were written the words: WELCOME TO BOTHER-IT'S-GONE.

"We'll wait 'til they're out of sight," said the Christmas Pig. "Then sneak into town and try and find a toy who might know DP . . ."

Once the carriages had disappeared, they hurried up the trail and into Bother-It's-Gone.

The new town was nothing like Disposable. Everything was clean and well tended. The snow-covered houses were all as snug, neat, and pretty as if they were made of gingerbread, their front doors painted in different colors. The roads had been swept clear, and multicolored Christmas lights were gleaming in more fir trees.

In spite of being cold and shivery in his pajamas, Jack felt his spirits rise. He could just imagine DP living in one of these little houses. It definitely seemed like a place where Things that were loved would be sent.

"Let's try this way," said the Christmas Pig, pointing up a side street.

It really was the prettiest little town Jack had ever seen. Through the snowy windows of the houses, he glimpsed roaring fires and cuckoo clocks, thick rugs and comfy armchairs. The Things they passed—a school tie and some exercise books, a fountain pen and an old button—looked far more cheerful than those back in Disposable. Jack was sure these Things must be valued Up There in the Land of the Living, to have been sent to live in such a nice, cozy place, yet he couldn't see any toys.

Finally, he spotted a black chess piece, who was standing talking to a large old-fashioned address book, whose cover was decorated with roses.

"Let's ask the chess piece if he's seen DP!" Jack said to the Christmas Pig.

"Hmm," said the Christmas Pig. "I'm not sure. A chess piece isn't really a toy."

"He's the closest Thing we've seen," said Jack.

"Well, all right," said the Christmas Pig. "But don't—"

"—mention having a cartoon, I know, I know!" said Jack.

So they drew into a doorway to wait for the chess piece and the address book's conversation to end.

". . . in *five minutes' time*, Mr. Knight, all right?" the address book was saying, in a voice that rang all the way down the street. "*Naughty* Mr. Knight, I shan't let you miss another one! We're starting in the Main Square and I *won't* take no for an answer! The tour will finish up at the Town Hall, where the mayor's most *graciously* agreed to show us round! Five minutes, Mr. Knight, don't forget or I'll be very upset!"

Laughing gaily, the address book bustled off, leaving the chess piece behind. As soon as she'd disappeared, the chess piece started to hop off in the other direction, going so fast that Jack and the Christmas Pig had to run to catch up.

"Excuse me?" said Jack.

"Yes?" panted the chess piece, coming to a halt. His top part was shaped like a horse's head.

"Have you seen a toy pig?" asked Jack. "He's about the same

size as this pig, but he's grayish, his ears are wonky, and his eyes are buttons."

"No, haven't seen any pig like that. You don't get a lot of toys in Bother-It's-Gone," said the chess piece. "Now excuse me, please, I'm trying not to get roped into another one of Addie's tours."

With these words, he gave a little whinny and hopped off again, disappearing into one of the snow-topped chalets and slamming the door behind him.

ADDIE THE ADDRESS BOOK

Jack was very disappointed to hear that there weren't many toys in Bother-It's-Gone. Where could DP have been sent, then? But before he and the Christmas Pig could discuss it, a loud whistle made them both jump. Jack was scared the whistle was some kind of alarm to tell the citizens of Bother-It's-Gone that some Thing was there that shouldn't be. However, the whistle was followed by the unmistakeable sound of a steam train approaching.

"Interesting," said the Christmas Pig, wrinkling up his snout again. "Where's the train come from? Let's go and have a look."

So Jack and the Christmas Pig hurried off in the direction of the train noises, and were just in time to see it arrive in a little station in the middle of town. The train was royal blue and gold, and once it had chugged to a halt in another cloud of steam, the doors opened and several Things tumbled out, including a gold wristwatch, a silver cup, and a bronze medal trailing a frayed ribbon.

"Look, it's her again," said the Christmas Pig, pointing a trotter. "That address book."

Sure enough, there she stood with her rose-patterned cover, handwritten pages swishing away the steam from the train.

She spoke at the top of her voice, as before. "How *wonderful* to see you all! You're in luck! *Just* in time for one of Addie's famous walking tours! *Such* a wonderful way to find out all about Bother-It's-Gone! Follow me, follow me, do!"

Jack could tell the new Things thought they had to do as Addie said, even though she wasn't wearing a Loss Adjuster's hat, and so they fell into step behind her.

"I think we should follow," said the Christmas Pig, "and try and find out where that train came from—but let's be careful. There's something about that address book I don't like."

So they followed Addie and the Things that had just come off the train to a little square, where a further collection of Things was waiting for the start of the tour. Jack saw the Pokémon card, Fingers, and Lunchy among them, all looking cheerful now that they'd seen what a pretty little town they'd come to live in.

"Allow me to introduce myself!" cried Addie, rustling to the front of the crowd. "My full name's Address Book, but you must call me Addie! As a *long*-standing resident of Bother-It's-Gone, and a *close* personal friend of the dear mayor, I like to conduct these little tours, to help everyone feel at home! Follow me, please, and if you've got any questions, don't *hesitate* to ask!"

CHAPTER 26

She bustled off up a new street and everyone followed. Jack and the Christmas Pig found themselves walking beside the gold watch they'd just seen get off the train.

"Just arrived?" asked the watch as he wriggled along.

"Yes," said the Christmas Pig.

"Didn't see you on the train."

"No," said the Christmas Pig. "We were Adjusted from Disposable."

"Ah," said Watch. "That would explain it."

The wristwatch had words engraved on his back, Jack noticed: *To Bob, with love, from Betty.*

"Are you looking at my inscription?" the watch asked Jack.

"Um—yes," said Jack, hoping it wasn't rude to look at a Thing's inscription.

"Huh," sighed the wristwatch. "Well, Betty and Bob don't love each other anymore, I know that much. The moment they told me I was being Adjusted, I thought 'they've split up.' Solid gold, I am, and Bob was very upset when he first lost me. But something must have changed, Up There. Bob clearly doesn't miss me as much as he did at first, or they wouldn't have made me move out of—"

"No talking at the back there!" cried Addie. "Or you won't get the full benefit of my tour! Now, we're just passing a *rather* nice chalet, one of the best in town—and it so happens to be mine!" she said, with a peal of laughter. "And here to our left, the residence of a *rather* charming silver-plated bookmark. *So* important to have well-bred, well-read neighbors! The previous occupant was a grubby old school timetable!" she added, with a shudder. "*What* a dreadful impression it gave newcomers, to see *him* as soon as they arrived!

"Now, for those of you who've come here straight from Mislaid," Addie went on, leading them round a corner, "I should explain that there are two towns in the Land of the Lost: Disposable and Bother-It's-Gone!"

The hands on the watch's face bunched up at these words, giving him a puzzled expression.

"No, madam," he called out to Addie, from the back of the crowd, "I think you've been misinformed. Medal, Cup, and I were sent here from—"

"There are only two towns in the Land of the Lost!" cried Addie, coming to a sudden halt and wheeling about to face the crowd, who all stopped so abruptly that some of them bumped into one another, and the silver cup toppled over and had to be helped upright again by a pair of furry mittens.

"Two towns!" repeated Addie, glowering around at them all. "One for the Good Things and one for the Bad! Disposable is for *worthless* objects, ones that are easy to replace, whose loss is barely noticed in the Land of the Living! But Bother-It's-Gone is for *special* Things. Every Thing in Bother-It's-Gone caused our humans a great deal of trouble when we were lost. We are valued. We are *important.* I, for instance," continued Addie, "spent fifty whole years in the possession of a lady Up There! She wrote the names and addresses and telephone numbers of her family and friends inside me. I was the only place she kept this important information!"

Addie flicked her pages and everyone saw the dense, spidery writing of the old lady.

"*Imagine* the trouble it caused when she lost me!"

Instead of looking sad, Addie burst into uncontrollable laughter.

"DP definitely isn't here," whispered Jack to the Christmas Pig. "Not if this is a place for Things that are glad they made their owners sad!"

A low voice spoke suddenly in Jack's ear, making him jump.

"One thing I must beg of you, dear laddie:

Please don't judge us all by horrid Addie."

Jack looked round. A grubby sheet of paper with eyes and a mouth doodled at the top had joined the walking tour.

As they all set off again, Jack asked the paper, "Who are you?"

"My name is Poem. See my scribbled lines?"

She unfurled slightly to show them the words scrawled across her.

"And as I'm verse, I only speak in rhymes."

"Oh," said Jack. "Have you just arrived here, too?"

"No, I've been here ages, but today

I thought I'd join the walking tour. I'll pay

A price for joining in, because you see

There's nobody old Addie hates, like me."

"Why does she hate you?" asked Jack.

"Because she's very mean and underhand,

And I'm not scared to say so, so I'm banned."

Sure enough, at that very moment, Addie, who'd just stopped outside a building with a little clocktower and double doors of polished wood, turned to talk to the crowd again and at once spotted Poem lurking at the back.

"Poem!" she cried. "Run along, now, dear, the mayor *told* you you're not allowed on my walking tours anymore!"

"Oh, sorry to intrude, that slipped my mind!" said Poem, grinning at Jack.

"Goodbye, dear, truthful Addie! You're so *kind!"*

Poem drifted away. Addie hitched her wide smile back onto her flowery face and said, "A little tip for newcomers: you should avoid Poem—she's mad, *quite* mad. And she lives with somebody even madder! I've been trying to get them both Adjusted to Disposable, but no luck so far. Now, I'm going to knock on the town hall's door, and if we're very lucky, the dear mayor will show us—"

But before Addie could knock, a square cheese grater came bursting out of the double doors, almost knocking Addie over. He was wearing a smart black tricorn mayor's hat, and behind him came an assortment of Loss Adjusters who looked slightly different to the usual kind. All wore black balaclavas, with the usual "L" badge on the forehead. Even though most of their faces were concealed, it was still easy to see what kind of Things they were. One was a magnifying glass, another was a net, and the third was an enormous hobnail boot.

"Oh no," whispered the Christmas Pig. "It's the Capture Team!"

"Trouble!" roared the mayor, who was brandishing a piece of paper. "The rumors are true! There are Things down here that shouldn't be! I've just received a description: a cuddly pig and an action figure in pajamas!"

MAYOR CHEESE GRATER

The mayor had barely finished saying "pajamas" when the Christmas Pig seized Jack's arm and tugged him sideways up an alleyway. There being nowhere else to hide, the Christmas Pig snatched the lid off a shiny silver dustbin with the mayor's coat of arms on it, and both he and Jack jumped inside, pulling the lid back over themselves. Jack was so scared it took him a moment to notice how very clean the empty dustbin was: apparently, even the insides of bins were regularly polished in Bother-It's-Gone.

"Settle down, settle down!" they heard the mayor shout, because the crowd had begun talking loudly at his announcement. When there was silence again, the mayor said, "Now, listen! That pig and action figure are breaking the law, and when the law gets broken, it gives the Loser an excuse to break the law back! Ten years ago, to this very day, the Loser came crashing into Bother-It's-

Gone, kicking in the fronts of houses and lifting off roofs, and it's not going to happen again, not on my watch!"

"W-why did he come here last time?" said a terrified voice that Jack recognized as Lunchy's.

"Because the last mayor broke the law!" shouted the cheese grater. "Mayor Pinking Shears was her name! She felt sorry for Surplus, so she let some of it sneak off the Wastes to hide in our attics! The Loser got wind of what she was up to and he ran into town, smashing apart houses! He scooped up all the Surplus and ate it, and gobbled up a few Things that had done nothing wrong, as well, and last of all he grabbed Pinking Shears and took her off to his lair, screaming as she went, and she's never been seen again!

"That's when I became mayor," roared the cheese grater, "and from that moment on, the law's been kept! Once a week, the Loss Adjusters and I conduct a *thorough* search of this town, to make sure there's no Thing here that shouldn't be! Right, everyone go straight home, and no loitering! Addie will tell newcomers where their houses are—you're to stay indoors until I give the all clear!"

Jack and the Christmas Pig remained squashed up in the bin, which was a very tight fit, listening to the crowd dispersing.

"What if the gold watch tells them he saw us?" whispered Jack. "Or the poem? Or *Lunchy*?"

"Then we'll be in deep trouble," the Christmas Pig whispered back. "But they all seemed like good Things. Hopefully, they won't tell."

After a few minutes, the tramp of Things heading home had

faded away. Now all that remained were the voices of the mayor and the Capture Team.

"They wouldn't be stupid enough to come right into the center of town," said the mayor confidently. "I suggest we spread out and work from the outside in."

The Capture Team agreed and they heard them moving away, calling to other Loss Adjusters to come and help search. The loudest noise of all came from the hobnailed boot, which made a menacing metal clunk with every step it took.

"That boot's name's Crusher," the Christmas Pig whispered in Jack's ear. "One of your socks told me about him. He's a favorite of the Loser's. Crusher's allowed to stamp all over Things if he catches them. After that, even if they're found, they're too broken to be of any use."

Jack slightly wished the Christmas Pig hadn't told him this.

"Did you hear what that watch started saying, before Addie stopped him?" the Christmas Pig went on.

"Yes," said Jack. "He came from a third town."

"Which makes sense," said the Christmas Pig, "because—"

"There were three doors in Mislaid!"

"Exactly," said the Christmas Pig.

"So DP must be in the last town!" said Jack.

"Yes, he must," said the Christmas Pig. "You know, I think our best hope is to try and sneak onto that train and hide, and let it take us to the other town. But we'll wait until dark. We've got no chance if we get out now."

And so they waited for nightfall.

At last, when they thought it was dark enough, they tried to get out of the bin, but somehow they'd become wedged in together. After a lot of wriggling, Jack managed to clamber out, and then he had to tug quite hard on the Christmas Pig's trotters until he came free, and they both toppled over onto a pile of snow, the Christmas Pig on top of Jack.

"Thank you," panted the Christmas Pig. "Sorry about that. My beans had settled."

"It's okay," said Jack, who was now both chilly and wet again. He got up, brushed himself down, and they crept off in the direction of the station, making sure to keep to the shadows.

They'd only gone a short distance when the mayor's voice came booming suddenly over loudspeakers on every corner. "Attention, all Things! Attention, all Things! We believe the Surplus pig and action figure have moved into the center of town under cover of darkness! Bolt your doors! Shutter your windows! Anybody helping the Surplus will be given to the Loser!"

Everywhere Jack and the Christmas Pig looked, the jewel-bright patches of light from the curtained windows were blacked out, and they heard the clicks of hundreds of bolts being driven home. When Mayor Cheese Grater had repeated his warning a second time, a ringing silence fell over the town of Bother-It's-Gone. The Things that lived there seemed suddenly too scared even to talk inside their own houses.

Jack's breath made a cloud of mist in the icy air as they stole ever closer to the station. Shivering, he realized he'd left his blanket behind in the mayor's bin, but all he cared about now was getting out of Bother-It's-Gone, which no longer felt a friendly, cozy place at all.

The station was in sight, just across the road, when they heard a rough voice up ahead. The Christmas Pig pulled Jack into a dark doorway and Jack held his breath, so the mist wouldn't give them away.

"You four—follow Spyglass to the western section. You lot—go with Net and search the east. The rest of you, follow me."

Jack heard the Loss Adjusters setting off in different directions, and again, the loudest noise of all was the stomping of the gigantic hobnail boot called Crusher.

When at last the sounds had died away once more, Jack and the Christmas Pig crept out of their hiding place and headed into the station.

But all Jack's hopes were dashed: the toy train had gone.

"Oh no—now what?" Jack whispered through his chattering teeth.

"Now," said a low menacing voice right behind them, "*it's crushing time.*"

CRUSHER

Jack and the Christmas Pig whirled around and at once, Jack realized that Crusher the hobnail boot had tricked them: he'd stamped in place to make them think he'd gone away. The boot came hopping nearer, and he was soon so close that Jack could see how two of his shoelace holes had become cruel little eyes. As the nails in his sole glinted in the moonlight, Jack thought suddenly of Mum. If he were stamped on and broken by Crusher, he'd never see her again. Without realizing what he was doing, Jack reached out and grabbed the Christmas Pig's trotter.

"Wait!" the Christmas Pig begged Crusher, gripping Jack's hand in return.

"What for?" sneered the boot, hopping nearer.

"For . . . for the thing that's about to happen!" said the Christmas Pig.

"What thing?" growled Crusher.

"The thing," said the Christmas Pig, "that will change everything! You won't want to miss it! Wait—just wait—"

CHAPTER 28

And then, to Jack's utter amazement, a shaft of golden light suddenly fell from the dark sky above, so that Crusher stood in a spotlight. The boot froze, then tried to escape the light, but it was no use: the column of gold began dragging him upward toward the Land of the Living.

"How did you do that?" Jack gasped to the Christmas Pig.

"I didn't!" said the pig, looking quite as stunned as Jack felt. "But sometimes waiting works!"

"Crusher's been found!" they heard one of the Loss Adjusters cry from a neighboring street.

"They're here!" yelled the boot, struggling furiously to escape the column of light carrying him higher and higher over the snowy rooftops. "They're *here*, right beside the st—"

But his voice was drowned out by the other Loss Adjusters, who were shouting congratulations at their old friend.

"Good for you, Crusher!"

"We'll miss you, old chum!"

"Happy booting, buddy!"

"Never mind the fond farewells!" shouted the grating voice of the mayor. "Keep searching—we've got Surplus to catch!"

Jack and the Christmas Pig had just started to run up the nearest dark street when a dim light appeared to their left. A door had flown open, and an urgent voice said:

"Quickly! Come inside—you'll thank me later!
We can hide you—"

POEM AND PRETENSE

Without pausing to consider whether it was sensible to obey the voice or not, Jack and the Christmas Pig hurtled through the open door, which closed behind them.

"*—from that dreadful grater!*" finished Poem.

The hall of the house was dimly lit. Poem's scribbled lines were barely visible.

"You aren't going to give us to the Loser, are you?" Jack whispered.

"What kind of traitor do you take me for?

You needed help, so I opened my door!"

"Sorry," said Jack, "I didn't mean—"

"We're very thankful," the Christmas Pig assured the poem.

Poem smiled.

"No harm done, dears. Suspicion's common sense!

Now come into the parlor—"

They followed Poem into a small sitting room.

"*—meet Pretense.*"

Draped in a seat beside the fire was the strangest Thing Jack had yet seen in the Land of the Lost. In fact, he couldn't make out whether it was a Thing, a person, or a ghost.

He had the shape and look of a teenage boy (though shrunk to the size of Jack and the Christmas Pig), and you could see right through him. Gold medals hung around his neck and he had a lipstick kiss on his cheek; he was dressed like a rock star, with a black leather jacket and pointed boots. When he saw Jack and the Christmas Pig, this strange Thing jumped up and said, "Hi! My friends at my old school called me Rebel. I've got a girlfriend who lives in another town. She's really pretty. We kiss a lot. These are the medals I've won for karate. I could kill you right now with my bare—"

"*Now's not the time, Pretense! Please save your lies!*" said Poem sternly.

"*These Things are running from the Loser's spies!*"

Pretense scowled. "You can talk about lying! You're completely made up!"

"*Great poems tell the truth—your fibs aren't art!*" said Poem in a dignified voice. Turning to Jack and the Christmas Pig she added,

"*He can't help lying, but he's good at heart!*"

Pretense glowered and kicked the edge of the rug. "I *could* kill someone with my bare hands, if I wanted," he mumbled sulkily. "I *could.*"

"Please sit down by the fire, get warm and dry," Poem told Jack and the Christmas Pig, ignoring her housemate.

"And then we'd like to help, Pretense and I."

"This is very kind of you," said the Christmas Pig.

"Yes, it is," said Jack. "Thank you."

He took the armchair nearest the fire and stretched out his freezing hands and feet to the flames. Being made of paper, Poem was staying well away from the fire, but Pretense slumped back down in his chair and said, "Poem told me she'd met you two on one of Addie's walking tours. I *hate* that address book. She's an even bigger liar than I am!"

"Pretense, you never spoke a truer word," said Poem approvingly.

"To hear her talk, you'd think she'd only heard
Of Disposable and Bother-It's-Gone.
Embarrassing, the way she carries on!"

"So there *is* another town, apart from Disposable and Bother-It's-Gone?" asked Jack.

"Of course! The one beyond the golden door!
Which Addie knows, of that you can be sure.
But Addie likes to think herself a queen—
The most important Thing there's ever been!
And so she tells herself it can't exist,
That wondrous place, the City of the Missed."

Jack and the Christmas Pig exchanged excited looks.

"The City of the Missed, did you say?" asked the Christmas Pig.

"That's right. We know it well, Pretense and I,
For once it was our home—I'm going to cry."

CHAPTER 29

Sure enough, a single tear leaked out of Poem's eyes and made an inky trickle down her page.

"Why aren't you still there?" asked Jack.

Poem moved a little closer to the fire and smoothed herself out to show them the many crossings-out and corrections all over her body.

"As you can see, I'm just an early draft,
Imperfect trial of my poet's craft!
And when she lost me, oh, her grief and rage!
'I need it back!' she stormed, 'that precious page!'
She swore my loss meant she could write no more!
And so they sent me through the golden door
And put me on a train of royal blue
And treated me with kindness, for they knew
How deeply I was missed—but soon that changed.
My poet tried again, she rearranged
My words, my rhymes, my meter—finally
She knew she'd made a better poem than me.
The Loss Adjusters came and brought me here
Where I'll remain forever, for I fear
I've now become a curiosity,
No longer does my poet cry for me."

As Poem wiped her inky eyes, Pretense sighed and said, "Poem and I have been friends since we met in the City of the Missed. My owner was a teenager. He had to move to a new school, miles away from all his old friends. He felt lonely, and frightened of that bully, Kyle Mason, so he made me. He pretended he could do karate and had a girlfriend and a cool nickname back in his old school . . . but the other teenagers soon saw through me. He didn't *want* to lose me: he was forced to. Losing me made *him* feel lost, at first. He missed me dreadfully, so I was sent through the golden door in Mislaid, just like Poem.

"But as time went on, my owner began to miss me less. He slowly realized it was better to tell the truth and have people like him for who he really was. That's when I was Adjusted and sent to Bother-It's-Gone. One day, I daresay, he'll be ashamed he ever had me at all, and when that day comes, I'll be shoved out onto the W—"

"What was that?" said the Christmas Pig, and Pretense fell silent. From a few chalets away came shouts and bangs.

"Uh-oh," said Pretense. "They're searching this street."

30

THE TUNNEL

"We've got to get to the City of the Missed!" said Jack. "Because—"

"Don't tell us why, it's safer far that way," said Poem. *"The less we know, the less we can betray."*

"Will the train be back soon?" asked the Christmas Pig.

"Not for hours," said Pretense. "Your best chance is to cross the Wastes of the Unlamented on foot, but that's very dangerous. The Loser has his lair in the middle of the Wastes, and he hunts Surplus by night. Of course," he added, perking up, "if I came with you, I could karate chop him to death—"

"Not now, Pretense, they're running out of time," said Poem. Turning to Jack and the Christmas Pig again, she said,

"You've just one hope: a secret friend of mine,
Though some may call her cracked, she's loyal and brave,
And many are the Things that she's helped save.
For I'll confess, now we're all safe inside,
You're not the only Surplus we've helped hide.

Sometimes, from the Wastes we give Things shelter
They need a break from running helter-skelter!
We've also sometimes helped Things run away,
It's crazy for a hunted Thing to stay
In Bother-It's-Gone, with our horrid mayor,
Who rules by fear and doesn't care what's fair.
And so I urge you both to trust my friend,
For she's a Thing on whom you can depend."

"When you say your friend's 'cracked'—" began Jack, worried.

"A little mad—but you two need a guide.
Without her you've no chance. Many have tried."

"Then please," said the Christmas Pig as the noises of the Loss Adjusters grew even closer and louder, "introduce us to your friend!"

Poem gestured for Jack and the Christmas Pig to follow her. Pretense jumped up, too, and came after them into Poem's bedroom.

"I *could* come with you—and I could get my girlfriend to help!"

"Just shift that rug and open the trapdoor," Poem told Pretense sternly.

"Then close it once we've gone. You know the score:
Do your favorite thing when the doorbell rings!
Pretend you've never seen these wanted Things!"

Pretense opened the trapdoor beneath a rug. Poem dropped into the hole beneath—being so light, she couldn't really hurt herself—whereas Jack and the Christmas Pig climbed down the ladder inside.

"Good luck!" Pretense called after them. "And I *do* have a girlfriend, and she's much prettier than Kyle Mason's!"

The trapdoor banged shut and Jack, the Christmas Pig, and Poem set off along a narrow tunnel that ran steeply downward, leading to the bottom of the mountain they'd climbed earlier on the wooden cart.

"Who made this tunnel, Poem?" asked the Christmas Pig.

"*A solid silver spoon, or so Things say,*" said Poem,

"*It happened long ago, before my day.*
He thought it quite beneath him, this small town,
And so, by night, he dug and dug, straight down.
The warnings of his friends that fool dismissed,
His only goal: the City of the Missed.
He never understood it's not your cost
That matters in the kingdom of the Lost,
But whether you once touched a human heart,
And how it hurt them when you had to part."

"And did the spoon reach the City of the Missed?" asked Jack hopefully.

"*He reached the Wastes of the Unlamented,*
Soon, his foolish plan the spoon repented,
A-hunting came the Loser 'cross the plain,
The silver spoon was never seen again."

The threesome continued down the steeply sloping tunnel in silence for a long time, until finally they reached a door in the rock, beside which hung a thick rope.

"*Now ring the bell. Old Compass won't be long,*

She always heeds the summons of my gong."

The Christmas Pig pulled the rope and a tinkling bell sounded on the other side of the door. After a few minutes, they heard something like a metal wheel turning over rock. The Christmas Pig opened the door a crack and Jack heard a hearty voice say, "More fugitives, eh, Poem?"

"Please help them cross the Wastes, my dear old friend.

Without your aid, they risk a gruesome end."

"'Course I'll 'elp, 'course I will!" said the merry voice. "You know 'ow much I loves adventures! Wantin' to go to the City of the Missed, I s'pose? Most Fings want to go there. Well, nicest city, innit?"

"We would like to go there, yes," said the Christmas Pig.

"Well, I can get you to the gates," said the voice, "but I can't get you inside. Will that do?"

"Yes, that's great," said Jack.

He and the Christmas Pig left the dark tunnel and stepped onto the Wastes of the Unlamented, at the foot of the mountain. The snow was falling thicker than ever.

Jack turned back to Poem. "Thank you, Poem."

She leaned down to whisper a final word in Jack's ear.

"The Loser hates the power of Christmas Eve.

He swears, once midnight chimes, you'll never leave."

"What?" said Jack, startled.

But Poem had already closed the door.

Part Five

THE WASTES OF THE UNLAMENTED

COMPASS

Compass, who stood balanced on her brass edge, was only half as tall as Jack and the Christmas Pig. Her glass was cracked and instead of pointing north, as it should have done, her pointer was hanging slightly askew.

Jack was so worried by what Poem had just whispered that instead of saying "hello" to her, he turned to the Christmas Pig and said, "Poem says once it's midnight Up There, I'll never be able to leave the Land of the Lost!"

"Yeah, I've 'eard that rumor, too," said Compass, before the Christmas Pig could answer. "The Loser finks if 'e can stop you two being found before midnight, 'e'll get to keep you forever and ever. I don't know why, because that's not 'ow it usually works. Lost is lost and found is found, don't matter when any of it 'appens."

But Jack had an awful feeling he knew why the Loser believed this, and he could tell by the expression on the Christmas Pig's face that he did, too. If Christmas Eve was the one night in the year a living boy could get into the Land of the Lost, mightn't it also be the only night when a boy could *return* to the Land of the Living? But as Jack couldn't say any of this out loud without revealing to Compass that he was human, he kept quiet.

"What're your names, then?" Compass asked, looking from one to the other.

"I'm Christmas Pig," said the Christmas Pig, "and this is Pajama Boy. He's an action figure."

"With the power of sleep and dreams," said Jack.

"Hm," sniffed Compass. "Well, you won't be getting much of either tonight. Sleeping's asking for trouble. Off we go, then!"

And without further ado, she rolled off so fast that Jack and the Christmas Pig had to jog to keep up, slipping and sliding over the snowy rubble of the Wastes. Jack's bare feet were soon very sore from running over the sharp, icy stones.

"Now, I've gotta warn you, there's some very strange Fings out 'ere on the Wastes," Compass called back to them. "Some of 'em are nearly as bad as the Loser 'imself!"

"Really?" said Jack nervously.

"Oh, yeah. See, nobody cares these Fings 'ave gone—in fact, some of 'em were lost on purpose, and I can't blame their owners! Some Fings really ain't worth keeping!"

She came to a sudden halt and turned to look at them, frowning. "'Oo's rattling?"

"Oh, that's me," said the Christmas Pig, who'd been clutching his stomach as usual, trying to stop his beans jumping around. "I've got beans in my stomach."

"Well, keep 'em as quiet as possible, won't you?"

"I'll try," said the Christmas Pig, gripping his tummy even harder.

They jogged off again. Compass's metal edge made so much racket rolling over the flinty ground that Jack thought it a bit unfair for her to tell off the Christmas Pig for his tummy beans. As though she'd read his mind, Compass called back to them, "It ain't ideal, being made of brass, because the Loser's got very sharp 'earing, but to tell the truth, I quite enjoy the thrill of it when 'e shows up! Don't worry, though," she added, seeing Jack's frightened glance at the Christmas Pig, "nobody's ever been eaten while they've been with me! I *love* cheating the Loser out of captures. 'E *'ates* me, you know."

"How were you lost, Compass?" panted the Christmas Pig.

"Dropped by a backpacker," said Compass cheerfully. "As a matter of fact, that was the second time 'e'd dropped me. The first time, 'e cracked my glass and knocked my needle off its pivot, and I didn't work very well after that, so when 'e lost me again in a jungle, 'e didn't even bother looking for me. Now I'm rusting away at the foot of a banana tree, and I doubt I'll ever be found. 'Oo'd want a broken compass?"

"But you *do* know the way to the City of the Missed?" panted Jack. He already had a stitch in his side, because he was running so fast.

"Oh yeah, don't worry about that," said Compass airily, "although we might zigzag a bit, to keep life interesting. Anyway, I've found new ways of guiding Fings since I arrived on the Wastes. Can you guess what they are?"

CHAPTER 31

"No," said the Christmas Pig, who was hurrying along as fast as his lower trotters could carry him.

"I make up stories with morals and I invent mottos. Would you like to 'ear one of my mottos?"

"Yes, please," panted Jack, because he could tell that was what Compass wanted him to say.

"'Nor' nor' west is all very well, but only the wise go sideways,'" said Compass proudly.

Jack didn't understand this at all, so he was glad when the Christmas Pig said, "Very true."

"It is, isn't it?" said Compass, sounding pleased. "And I can tell you a story with a moral, if you'd like."

"Oh, yes, please," said the Christmas Pig breathlessly.

"There were once three compasses," said Compass, "a big one, a medium-sized one, and a tiny one. The big one led the way up a mountain, and the medium-sized one steered a boat across the sea, but the tiny one got dropped in a vegetable patch. And the moral of that is, 'never make friends with a radish.'"

Jack and the Christmas Pig both made interested and impressed noises, which seemed to please Compass, and on they ran over snowy rock and loose stones, and the stitch in Jack's side hurt more than ever.

They struggled on through the chilly darkness for what felt like hours. Every so often, Jack or the Christmas Pig would stumble and the other would help him up again. Their sleep inside Lunch Box seemed a very long time ago, but Jack was too frightened to be tired. Every now and then, he'd see shapes looming up in the darkness and worry that they were the Loser, or some of the strange Things Compass had warned them about, but when they got closer, it was always clumps of thistles.

"Where's your blanket?" said the Christmas Pig, noticing Jack shivering in his pajamas.

"I left it in the bin by mistake," panted Jack. "I'm fine."

If only they could get safely across the Wastes without being eaten by the Loser, they'd find DP. The thought of hugging Dur Pig's familiar squishy body and breathing in his friendly smell kept Jack running, in spite of the cold and his sore feet.

Then a horrible moan came echoing across the Wastes.

"Was that the Loser?" gasped Jack in panic. "Is he coming? Should we hide?"

"No," said Compass, still bowling along. "That's a Pain."

"A what?" said Jack.

"A Pain," repeated Compass. "An 'uman Pain. Of course, their owners are delighted to get rid of Pains, so they end up 'ere on the Wastes, roaming around in packs and 'owling. I feel quite sorry for them, really. It can't be much fun being a—"

Compass rolled to a sudden halt again. Two dark shapes had appeared ahead of them, blocking their path.

THE BROKEN ANGEL

The outlines of the shapes looked like a mother and a child to Jack, but he didn't trust his senses anymore and he drew close to the Christmas Pig.

"'Oo goes there?" shouted Compass.

"Who're you?" called a frightened lady's voice.

Out of the darkness walked a Christmas angel. One of her wings was badly bent, her plum-and-gold dress was torn, and she was hiding her face behind her left hand. The little blue bunny they'd watched being forced down the chute in Mislaid was leading her along. He was as filthy as ever, his fur clogged with earth.

"Why are you 'iding your face?" Compass asked the angel suspiciously.

"Because you'll run away if I show you," said the angel. "Every Thing I've shown has fled, except for Blue Bunny."

"This is no time for concealment," said Compass sternly. "'Ow do I know you're not one of the Loser's spies?"

The angel lowered her hand. Her head was cracked, her face broken. One of her eyes was missing. There was a great puncture hole in her cheek. When she heard Jack gasp, a tear leaked from her remaining eye. She covered her face again and began to cry.

"I know I'm ugly!" she sobbed. "A dog got me!"

But Jack hadn't gasped because he didn't like her face. He'd gasped because he'd just recognized her. That purple-and-gold dress, those chipped curls, those glittery, plastic wings—this was *their* Christmas Angel, the one Gran had chosen, and which Toby-the-dog had eaten. What Jack couldn't understand was why she was down here, in the Land of the Lost, if Toby-the-dog had destroyed her . . .

"Being broken's not reason enough to get sent to the Wastes," said Compass, sounding even more suspicious. "There's plenty of chipped and cracked Things 'oo're so precious their owners won't let 'em out of their sight!"

"I was never precious to the family at all!" said Broken Angel, trying to stem her tears. "I was bought to replace an angel they loved! Bought in a hurry because the shops were crowded—the family didn't like me even when they bought me, I could tell!"

Jack felt horribly guilty. At least the angel had her hand back over her remaining eye, so she couldn't recognize him.

"They put me on the top of the tree, but none of the other decorations were friendly," she sobbed. "They were all mourning the loss of the old angel, who was their friend and their leader! And then—then—"

"The dog pulled over the tree," said Jack, without thinking.

"Yes!" gasped Broken Angel in surprise. "How did you know?"

"I guessed," said Jack quickly.

"The tree fell, and so did I. I got tangled in the branches. The dog tried to drag me out but I was stuck, so he chewed as much of me as he could reach. When the family found the tree knocked down, and saw bits of my dress and my face on the floor, they thought the dog had eaten me, like the old angel. They didn't notice me hanging upside down at the back. They stood the tree up again and there I am, lost among the branches, out of sight.

"Nobody misses me, nobody cares," said the angel, starting to weep again. "When they come to throw out the tree, they'll throw me out, too!"

The Christmas Pig stepped forward and put a trotter on the angel's shoulder, while the little bunny sadly stroked her remaining hand.

"I'm a Replacement, too," the Christmas Pig told her. "It might yet be all right. They might find you and fix you!"

"We need to get moving," said Compass, before the weeping angel could respond. "Tag along if you like," she added, to the angel and the blue bunny. "There's safety in numbers, but you'll need to keep up."

THE STORY OF THE BLUE BUNNY

And so they ran on. After a while, Jack noticed that the little blue bunny hopping along beside him was gazing up at him in admiration.

"I'm very sorry to stare," said Blue Bunny timidly, "but you're so new and detailed! You must have been expensive! I haven't seen any Thing as fine as you on the Wastes."

The blue bunny was a badly made little toy, with lopsided eyes and arms sewn on at odd angles.

"What are you, if it's not a rude question?" asked the toy now.

"An action figure," said Jack. "Pajama Boy, with the power of sleep and dreams. I've got my own cartoon," he added, because the Christmas Pig was now talking to Broken Angel, so couldn't hear.

"How wonderful," sighed Blue Bunny, his dark eyes shining. "But why are you on the Wastes? Surely your owner's looking for you everywhere?"

CHAPTER 33

"He's very spoiled," said Jack, repeating what the Christmas Pig had told Specs. "He's got lots of toys. He hardly noticed he'd lost us."

"That's awful," said the little bunny sadly. "I never thought a toy like *you* would be so badly treated. The likes of *me* don't expect much, but you're different. Your own cartoon! You're famous!"

"Didn't your owner like you?" asked Jack, because he didn't want more questions about his cartoon. He couldn't really think of any adventures that involved sleeping.

"No," sighed Blue Bunny. "He won me in a raffle at the fair. Every ticket won a prize. My owner wanted the football, but he got me instead. He groaned when they handed me to him, then stuffed me in his pocket and took me home. He never played with me. I lay on a shelf until one day, one of his friends visited. The friend threw me out of the open window into a flower bed, as a joke."

The bunny's voice broke.

"Nobody looked for me. Nobody cared. I lay in the flower bed for weeks. It rained. I was so cold, so wet, but I had no choice but to lie in the mud and wait."

"I don't understand," said Jack.

"I was stuck between two worlds, you see," said Blue Bunny. "It happens sometimes, if it isn't clear whether you've been thrown away or lost. I was stuck, belonging nowhere, frozen and dirty and waiting for my owner to remember me. If he believed me thrown away, I'd cease to exist. If he thought me lost, I would descend to the Land of the Lost. On Christmas Eve," Blue Bunny went on, "the boy was packing a cuddly toy to take to his grandparents' house and suddenly he remembered that I was lost, but he didn't care or think of looking for me. At that moment, my fate was sealed. I fell straight down here and the Loss Adjusters seized me. They shoved me down the chute that comes out in the middle of the Wastes. I was alone and very frightened, but after a while, I met Broken Angel. We've been wandering the Wastes together ever since. It's been nice to have somebody who understands how I feel. That might sound silly to a Thing like you—"

"No, it doesn't," said Jack. "I had a friend who always understood me, but then I lost him and it ruined everything . . ."

The Christmas Pig glanced back at Jack, an odd expression on his face. Afraid the Christmas Pig was about to tell him off for talking about DP, he changed the subject.

"Perhaps you'll be found by somebody else," Jack told the blue bunny. Through the swirling snow, he could see patches of darkness where no stars shone, which he was sure were openings onto the Land of the Living.

"No, I won't," sighed Blue Bunny. "My body's still in the garden, covered in mud, barely visible. The family's gone away for Christmas. There's nobody to find me now. I belong to the Loser, but Broken Angel and I have agreed to face the end together, and that's some comfort."

Jack felt very sorry and wished he could take the little blue bunny home to his own bedroom, but he was starting to learn the laws of the Land of the Lost and was sure this wouldn't be allowed.

CHAPTER 33

Then, before anyone could say another word, noises exploded out of the darkness around them.

"Danger!" yelled Compass, rolling back to them. "Stick together and brace yourselves! It's the Bad 'Abit gang!"

34
THE BAD HABITS

Compass, Jack, the Christmas Pig, Broken Angel, and Blue Bunny drew close together, back to back, as a swarm of dark shadows and fiery red dots began to circle them. Voices cackled and there was suddenly a nasty smell of smoke in the air.

"What are they?" asked Jack, very frightened. There seemed to be quite a number of the Things: the fiery red dots looked like eyes, and he could hear cackling and growling.

"I told you: Bad 'Abits!" said Compass. "Watch out, because they often throw—"

Splat! An enormous slimy something hit her.

"What's that?" squealed Blue Bunny.

"It's a booger!" said Compass furiously, scraping it off herself as she rolled on the spot. "I know that was you, Picker!"

The Things surrounding them howled with laughter and several more giant boogers came flying through the air, while Jack and the others tried to dodge them. *Splat, splat, splat* came the boogers. Then something hard and sharp hit Jack in the face and he yelped in pain.

"What happened?" asked the Christmas Pig.

"They threw something pointy at me," said Jack, looking down at the sharp yellow object shaped like a boomerang. "What is that?"

"A bit of Chewfinger's nail!" said Compass. "*Will you stop it!*" she shouted at the jeering gang surrounding them. "Or the Loser will 'ear us and we'll all be eaten!"

"That you, Compass?" said a raucous voice. "Who're you smuggling this time?"

The Things around them now drew closer. Jack half wished they'd remained hidden. They were even odder than Pretense and a lot scarier.

They all seemed to be bits of humans. Some were mouths: one was loudly chewing gum and others smoking stinking cigarettes, which made the glowing red dots and the nasty smell. There were noses, ears, a single finger, its nail chewed to a bloody stub, several oozing zits that were so disgusting Jack could barely look at them, and a couple of fists, which were pounding the ground in a menacing fashion as though they couldn't wait to start hitting someone.

"Still 'ere, Sugarguzzler?" Compass said to the biggest of the mouths. "You swore you'd be home for Christmas! Your owner didn't want you back, then?"

"Give him time, give him time," said the mouth, revealing blackened stumps of teeth. "There'll be chocolate and sweeties all around him now. He's bound to crack and start scarfing again."

"Hang on a minute," said a strangely familiar voice just behind Jack. "Don't I know you two?"

Jack's heart leapt. Even though he was furious at her, even though she'd thrown DP out of the car window, he'd never been so glad to hear that voice in his life. She belonged to home and the Land of the Living, and in that moment, all Jack could remember was how kind she'd once been, when he felt very small and lost.

"Holly!" he cried, spinning round.

But Holly was nowhere to be seen. Instead, he found himself facing a fist as big as he was.

"This is strange," said the fist, in Holly's voice.

"What is, Bullyboss?" asked a giant ear, in a sly voice. It slid closer. "I *love* hearing strange things."

"I'm down here because I chucked a toy pig like him out of a car window," said Bullyboss, in Holly's voice. "And you look a bit familiar, too . . ."

"He's an action figure!" said the Christmas Pig quickly. "Pajama Boy, with the power of sleep and dreams!"

"He's got his own cartoon!" piped up Blue Bunny.

The Bad Habits jeered.

"I bet it's rubbish," said Sugarguzzler.

"No wonder they don't care he's lost," sneered Picked Zit.

"Fine talk from you!" said the Christmas Pig. "Your owners were *glad* to get rid of you!"

"My owner will be back for me any moment," growled Bullyboss. "I'm her mate, I am. She needs me."

"Why does she need you?" asked Jack.

CHAPTER 34

"Because, *stupid*," said Bullyboss, "I make her feel better. Her mum wants her to get to the Olympics. Trouble is, Holly doesn't like gymnastics anymore. She wants to do music instead. She thinks her dad might understand, but he's been stolen by her new stepbrother. Well, I make that stepbrother pay, see? He's got everything, he has: a nice mum, and Holly's dad, and nobody making him win medals and telling him off if he doesn't . . . He deserves punishing . . . *that's* why I threw his stupid toy pig out of the car window . . ."

Jack was amazed. He'd never imagined Holly thought he was lucky . . .

"Only Holly feels really guilty now . . . She got rid of me and swore she'd never bully the boy again . . . but she will . . ."

"'Course she will, 'course she will," said the ear, in its nasty sly voice. "My owner's just the same. She was caught reading her sister's diary, and vowed she'd never sneak around and eavesdrop ever again—but how else is she going to find out secrets? Secrets are fun. Secrets are my favorite thing. Who wants to hear a good secret I heard today, when I was sneaking around on the outskirts of Bother-It's-Gone?"

All the Bad Habits clamored to hear the secret.

"I was sitting in a bush on the edge of the Wastes," said the ear. "It's a good place to hear things, because the Loss Adjusters patrol there to make sure no Surplus tries to sneak off the Wastes and up the mountain."

"Get on with it!" snarled Bullyboss.

"Well, they were talking about a couple of Things that are on the run," said Sneaky. "Things that shouldn't be down here in the Land of the Lost at all. And you know what those Things are?"

"What?" asked several of the mouths.

"A cuddly pig and an action figure!" said the ear. "*Exactly* like—"

But at that moment a gigantic *BOOM* echoed across the Wastes. The ground shuddered and all the Bad Habits screamed.

"The hunt's afoot!" shouted Compass gleefully. "It's the Loser! You four, stay with me! Now, RUN!"

THE LOSER

Compass rolled off very fast and the Bad Habits scattered, shrieking, into the darkness, as did Broken Angel and Blue Bunny, but for a few moments, Jack was so terrified he couldn't move at all.

Two gigantic white searchlights were moving through the sky above the Wastes. Their twin beams swept the ground, illuminating the many scurrying Things that were running pell-mell away from the Loser. The searchlights were his eyes, and they swung over the snowy wastes as the Loser turned his giant head this way and that. He was so tall that Jack could actually hear the top of his head scraping on the high wooden sky as his blinding eyes scanned the ground for Things to eat.

It was hard to tell whether he was a giant man or a robot. He didn't walk on feet, but on steel points like a two-legged spider. His body, his arms, and his legs were all covered in millions and millions of broken Things, so that he glistened all over with cogs, springs, handles, aerials, buttons, lids, and other bits of the bodies he'd torn to pieces before eating.

The Loser let out a terrible cry that shook the ground and made the boulders tremble. It was a howl of fury but also of anguish, as though he'd lost something he loved and would never, ever get back.

And then he swooped.

An enormous hand with fingers like steel girders swished across the Wastes, scooping up fleeing Things. Jack heard their screams as the Loser pulled them up into the air and examined them by the light of his pitiless eyes.

"Jack, MOVE!" shouted the Christmas Pig, seizing Jack's hand and tugging as the Loser stooped again. The giant steel fingers flew past once more, coming so close to where Jack was standing that he saw the jagged fingertips, encrusted with glass and steel.

Jack let the Christmas Pig pull him along, but his legs felt numb with terror and he kept tripping. The beams from the Loser's eyes were darting and flashing all around them, so that Jack became sick and dizzy and lost all sense of direction. At any moment, he was sure, he'd feel the giant metal hand of the Loser closing around him and yanking him up into the air.

"Where's Compass?" he cried as the Christmas Pig pulled him on.

"I don't know," shouted the Christmas Pig. "Just run, we've got to find somewhere to hide!"

The Loser screamed again and the spotlights of his eyes slid

past them, grazing Jack's elbow. Jack heard Holly's voice somewhere out in the darkness.

"Please no—please no—argh!"

"Jack, come on!" shouted the Christmas Pig, because Jack had stopped running and was trying to pull free of his grip.

"Holly!" said Jack. "He's got Holly!"

"It isn't Holly, you know it isn't Holly!" said the Christmas Pig, dragging Jack onward with both trotters. "It was Holly's bad habit and you should be glad it's gone!"

But Jack hated hearing Holly's voice so desperate and scared, and was only distracted when he spotted Broken Angel up ahead, running for her life, but stumbling over her torn dress, and unable to see properly through her only remaining eye.

"Take my free hand!" Jack called to her.

"Oh, thank you!" she cried.

But as she stretched her unbroken arm toward him, the beams from the Loser's eyes found her. The broken angel tripped, and the Loser pounced. His huge glittering fist seized her, and she was lifted up into the air.

"There's nothing we can do!" said the Christmas Pig fiercely as Jack tried to pull him backward. "Run, Jack, run, or it'll be us next!"

THISTLES

Lie flat!" said the Christmas Pig, pulling Jack behind a large clump of thistles, so they were hidden in shadow. Huddled together on the snowy ground they peered through the spiky leaves. The Loser's arms were now full of Things, and he was striding away from them, the ground shaking as he went.

"The angel, the poor angel!" gasped Jack through numb lips. If only he'd been faster at grabbing her hand, she might not have been taken! "What happens to them? What does he do to them? Perhaps we can rescue them!"

"We can't," said the Christmas Pig quietly. "He's taking them to his lair. That's where he tears them to pieces and sucks out the Alivened bit. Then, if he likes their bodies, he makes them part of his armor."

"But what if they were found, now, Up There?" said Jack.

"That would save them," said the Christmas Pig, "but nobody's looking, Jack. Nobody cares that they're lost—they're even glad to be rid of them. What human would want a Christmas angel that badly broken? Who'd want a nasty nose-picking habit?"

"But after the Loser sucks out the Alivened part, and breaks up their body and makes it part of his body, what happens to the Thing Up There?" asked Jack. "The angel's still tangled in the tree, isn't she?"

"Not for long," said the Christmas Pig. "Once the Loser has sucked out her Alivened part, she'll vanish Up There. There's no going back for a Thing that's eaten by the Loser. You're gone forever. It's what humans call death."

Jack was so cold, tired, and scared, he wanted DP so badly, and he felt so guilty about the angel, he couldn't keep back the tears any longer. He broke down. He tried not to make any noise, but he hadn't fooled the Christmas Pig, who put his trotters around Jack and pulled him close.

"We'll freeze unless we hug," said the pig gruffly. "We'll stay here—maybe get a few hours' sleep—and then, when it's light, we'll try and find a way to the City of the Missed."

"But how will we find our way without Compass?" asked Jack.

"I don't know yet," admitted the Christmas Pig. "But we'll think of something."

So Jack curled up beside the Christmas Pig, who cuddled him, and slowly Jack began to warm up. He was still scared and miserable, but at least he was warmer.

"Thanks, Christmas Pig," he said, after a while.

"You're welcome," said the Christmas Pig, sounding surprised.

After a short silence, Jack said, "It's a stupid name."

"What is?" asked the Christmas Pig.

CHAPTER 36

"'The Christmas Pig,'" said Jack. "It's too long. I wouldn't have called you that if I'd kept you. It isn't an everyday name."

"What would you have called me, then?" asked the Christmas Pig.

Jack thought for a while.

"Maybe 'CP,'" he said. "Which stands for 'Christmas Pig.'"

"'CP,'" said the Christmas Pig. "I like that."

"I could ask Holly to call you that, if you like," said Jack, yawning.

"What d'you mean?" said the Christmas Pig.

"When I give you to her," said Jack.

"I don't understand," said the Christmas Pig.

"You made me promise to give you to Holly when we get back from the Land of the Lost. Remember?"

"Oh," said the Christmas Pig. "Yes, I remember."

They lay for a while without talking, but Jack could tell that the Christmas Pig wasn't asleep.

"We'll still see each other," said Jack, now feeling drowsy, "when we get home. We might even all play together. You'll like DP."

"I'm sure I will," said the Christmas Pig. "We're brothers, after all."

"Yes," said Jack. "I didn't think so at first, but you're quite similar, really. D'you . . ." he yawned. "D'you think we'll find DP soon?"

"I'm sure we will," said the Christmas Pig. "You'll miss him forever, so he must be in the City of the Missed. It's the only place left to look."

"Yes," said Jack. He was on the very edge of sleep now, and he could almost imagine that he was cuddled up with DP beside him. The Christmas Pig didn't smell new anymore: he'd become grubby from hiding in the smelly lunch box and their long walk down the earthy tunnel to the Wastes.

"I can't wait to see DP. Won't he be surprised when he realizes I came all this way to rescue him?" said Jack.

"He'll be amazed," said the Christmas Pig. "No boy has done this for a toy, ever, in the history of the world."

Jack was on the very edge of sleep when he heard the rattling of the Christmas Pig's tummy beans again.

"Is the Loser coming?" he whispered.

"No," said the Christmas Pig. "Don't worry. Sleep."

Jack thought he heard a sniff.

"Are you all right, CP?"

"Of course I'm all right," said the Christmas Pig.

This was a relief, because for a moment, Jack had thought that the Christmas Pig was crying.

37

TRAIN TRACKS

The sun was rising on the high wooden ceiling that was the sky in the Land of the Lost. Although it was only painted, it shone brightly enough to wake Jack as he lay curled up behind the thistles on the Wastes.

It had stopped snowing, but was still very cold. The Wastes of the Unlamented stretched as far as he could see in every direction, covered in snow, the occasional clump of thistles swaying in a chilly wind. There was no sign of any Thing—not even the Christmas Pig.

Panicking, Jack struggled to his feet.

"CP?" he called. "CP, where are you?"

"It's all right, I'm here!" said the Christmas Pig, hurrying back into sight. "I've found something—come over here!"

He led Jack a short distance and pointed.

"Look. Railway tracks."

"They must lead to the City of the Missed!"

"Exactly," said the Christmas Pig. "The trouble is, without Compass, I don't know which direction to go in."

They looked up and down the railway tracks, but there was nothing to tell which way led to Bother-It's-Gone and which to the City of the Missed.

A noise behind them made them jump. They wheeled around to see the blue bunny, as grubby as ever, although tears had made clean streaks in his muddy fur.

"It's you!" he gasped. "Oh, I'm so glad the Loser didn't get you!" He hugged first Jack and then the Christmas Pig, which left both of them rather muddy.

"We're glad he didn't get you, either," said Jack.

"Where's Compass?" asked Blue Bunny.

"We don't know," said the Christmas Pig. "She rolled off into the dark, and we weren't fast enough to keep up."

"Oh dear," moaned Blue Bunny. "I hope she wasn't caught. And I'm so worried about Broken Angel. She told me to run as quick as I could, but when I looked back, I couldn't see her anymore. I've been searching for her all night. She was my best friend. Have you seen her?"

"No," said the Christmas Pig, with a warning look at Jack. "Blue Bunny, I don't suppose you know where these tracks lead, do you?"

"I'm afraid not," said Blue Bunny, considering the train tracks. "I'll tell you something strange, though. When the train is traveling that way"—he pointed toward the horizon which was still dark—"the Things on board look sad. But when the train is traveling in that direction"—he pointed toward the horizon that was glowing red and gold, from where the painted sun had risen—"the Things on board look happy."

CHAPTER 37

Jack looked at the Christmas Pig and could tell he was thinking exactly what Jack was: this surely meant that the Things traveling east, toward the place where the painted sun had risen, were journeying toward the City of the Missed rather than Bother-It's-Gone.

"I think we'll take a stroll this way," said the Christmas Pig, setting off along the train tracks toward the ever-lightening horizon.

"D'you mind if I come?" asked Blue Bunny.

"Of course not," said Jack kindly, so the bunny hopped after them.

THE CITY GATES

They walked for hours along the train tracks toward the horizon, and saw nothing ahead except more snow-covered ground and the tracks stretching into the distance. Jack kept glancing up at the painted sky. The Christmas Pig had said that a day here was an hour above in the Land of the Living and Jack couldn't help thinking about Poem's warning that they had to leave the Land of the Lost before Christmas Eve ended. The idea of being trapped down here forever, waiting for the Loser to catch him, was dreadful. But Jack was certain that if he found DP, then DP would make everything all right, just as he'd always done, so he kept walking as fast as he could along the train tracks, following the Christmas Pig.

The painted sun high above them slid slowly across the wooden sky and began to descend into more dark cloud. It started to snow again.

At last, the Christmas Pig stopped, his trotter shading his little black eyes.

CHAPTER 38

"Jack, can you see something?" he whispered. "Something . . . sparkling?"

Jack peered toward the horizon. Sure enough, in the far distance, he could see something glittering.

"Is it the sea?" he asked.

They walked a little farther and soon the misty outlines of a beautiful walled city took shape. They could see turrets and spires, and the golden roof of what looked like a palace.

At last they got near enough to make out a pair of golden gates in the city wall. They were engraved with the same vines and flowers as the golden door back in Mislaid. Now the train tracks were joined by a second set, which arrived from a different direction. Jack guessed the second tracks came directly from Mislaid, carrying the Things that had gone through the golden door.

The Christmas Pig held out a warning trotter.

"Loss Adjusters!" he whispered.

Sure enough, a dagger, a nail file, and a fierce-looking nutcracker were marching up and down in front of the gates. These Loss Adjusters were wearing the fanciest black hats Jack had yet seen: tall helmets with long black feathers sticking out of them, while the "L"s on the hats were made of gold.

Jack, the Christmas Pig, and Blue Bunny crouched down out of sight behind another clump of thistles, the snow settling on their heads and shoulders as they stared at the gates, trying to think of a plan.

"Perhaps," Jack whispered, "if we wait until the train comes along, we can jump onto the back of it?"

"It'll be going too fast," said the Christmas Pig. "You'd get injured."

"Wait—you're trying to *get in?*" asked Blue Bunny in amazement. Jack nodded.

"They'll never let you!" said Blue Bunny. "We're Surplus! We don't belong in such a fine place as that! That's where the Things that are truly missed go!"

"There's nothing very special about those gates," said the Christmas Pig, ignoring the blue bunny. "They seem quite ordinary. It's the Loss Adjusters who are the problem. They'll grab us and hand us to the Loser the moment we show ourselves. If only we had a decoy."

"Do you just want to live in nice houses?" asked Blue Bunny. "Or is there another reason you want to get in?"

"Yes," said Jack, before the Christmas Pig could stop him. "Somebody I need's in there. He's called DP and he's my favorite cuddly toy."

For a long moment, Jack and Blue Bunny stared into each other's eyes and then Blue Bunny let out a long sigh of amazement.

"You're a boy," he whispered. "You're real."

"He isn't," said the panic-stricken Christmas Pig. "He's an action figure called—"

"It's all right, Pig," said Blue Bunny, "I won't tell anybody, I promise. You really came all the way into the Land of the Lost to find your favorite toy?" he asked Jack, who nodded.

"Then I'll be your decoy," said Blue Bunny. "It would be an honor."

CHAPTER 38

And before either Jack or the Christmas Pig could stop him, the blue bunny scrambled out from their hiding place and gamboled right over to the Loss Adjusters, who all stopped marching up and down and stared at him.

"Hello there!" said the Blue Bunny. "Please, could I come and live in your city?"

"Don't be stupid," sneered the dagger, threatening to jab the bunny. Blue Bunny scampered away a short distance and tried again.

"Please let me in! I can do tricks!"

He tried to turn a somersault, but landed on his head, which crumpled his ears. The Loss Adjusters jeered, but they didn't even bother to chase him away.

Just then, there were several loud bangs over their heads. Everybody—Jack and the Christmas Pig, Blue Bunny and the Loss Adjusters—looked up. It sounded as though a gigantic ball was bouncing across the high painted ceiling. This was the first time that Jack had heard a noise from the Land of the Living. There were very few finding holes over the Wastes of the Unlamented, but it so happened that one of them lay directly overhead.

Then, from a long, long way away, came a little girl's voice. She had an accent Jack didn't recognize.

"My ball's gone over the hedge! It's in next door's garden!"

"Squeeze through and get it, then, Jeanie," said a lady's voice.

Jack, the Christmas Pig, the Loss Adjusters, and Blue Bunny continued to stare up at the big hole in the wooden sky, across which footsteps now echoed. Then they heard the little girl's voice again, louder and clearer than before.

"It landed in a flower bed! I'm glad they're not home."

And then a golden shaft of light appeared and hit the little bunny, who stood transfixed, his mouth open, a wild hope gleaming in his dark eyes.

"Mum!" said the girl's voice. "I've found a bunny! A blue bunny in the flower bed!"

The grubby blue bunny rose a few inches off the ground, tugged upward by the golden light. He looked around in amazement, clearly unable to believe what was happening.

"Leave it where you found it, Jeanie!" said the mother far above them. "It'll belong to one of the boys!"

"It must have been here for ages and ages!" said the little girl's voice. "It's all covered in mud!"

Blue Bunny rose a little higher in the shaft of golden light. Now he was hanging in midair. The three Loss Adjusters who were supposed to be guarding the gate were all so astonished to see what was happening that they walked forward to get a better view of the hole above them, trying to catch a glimpse of the girl odd enough to like a muddy blue bunny.

"Mum, they've left him out here for weeks, they can't care about him! Please can I—"

"Jeanie, no, not if it belongs to one of the boys," said the mother's voice.

Now the nutcracker, the nail file, and the dagger were standing right beneath the suspended bunny, clearly astounded that a Thing so dirty and badly made might have a chance of being found.

"Jack, now," whispered the Christmas Pig. "Run."

CHAPTER 38

"But—"

"It's our only chance!" said the pig. "We can get through the gates while they're watching the bunny!"

So Jack got slowly to his feet, then dashed toward the glittering gates, and the Christmas Pig followed, holding his tummy.

Still the bunny hung, suspended in golden light, between the Land of the Living and the Land of the Lost, and the Loss Adjusters stood openmouthed beneath him, gazing upward.

"Please, Mum," said the little girl's voice. "*Please* let me keep him. We'll wash him and show him to the boys and if they want him back, I'll give him to them."

"They won't want me back!" cried Blue Bunny in desperation. "Oh, take me, please take me, let me be yours!"

But of course, neither the girl nor her mother could hear the bunny.

"Look at his sweet little face, Mum!" said the girl.

Jack heard a tiny clink behind him. The Christmas Pig had pushed open the golden gates. Jack slid through them, still looking back over his shoulder at the bunny.

"Oh, *all right*," came the mother's voice, half-amused, half-exasperated. "I just hope he doesn't clog up the washing machine!"

And with a sudden whoosh, Blue Bunny was whipped through the hole and out of the Land of the Lost, but not before waving a single muddy paw at Jack, a look of bewildered joy on his face.

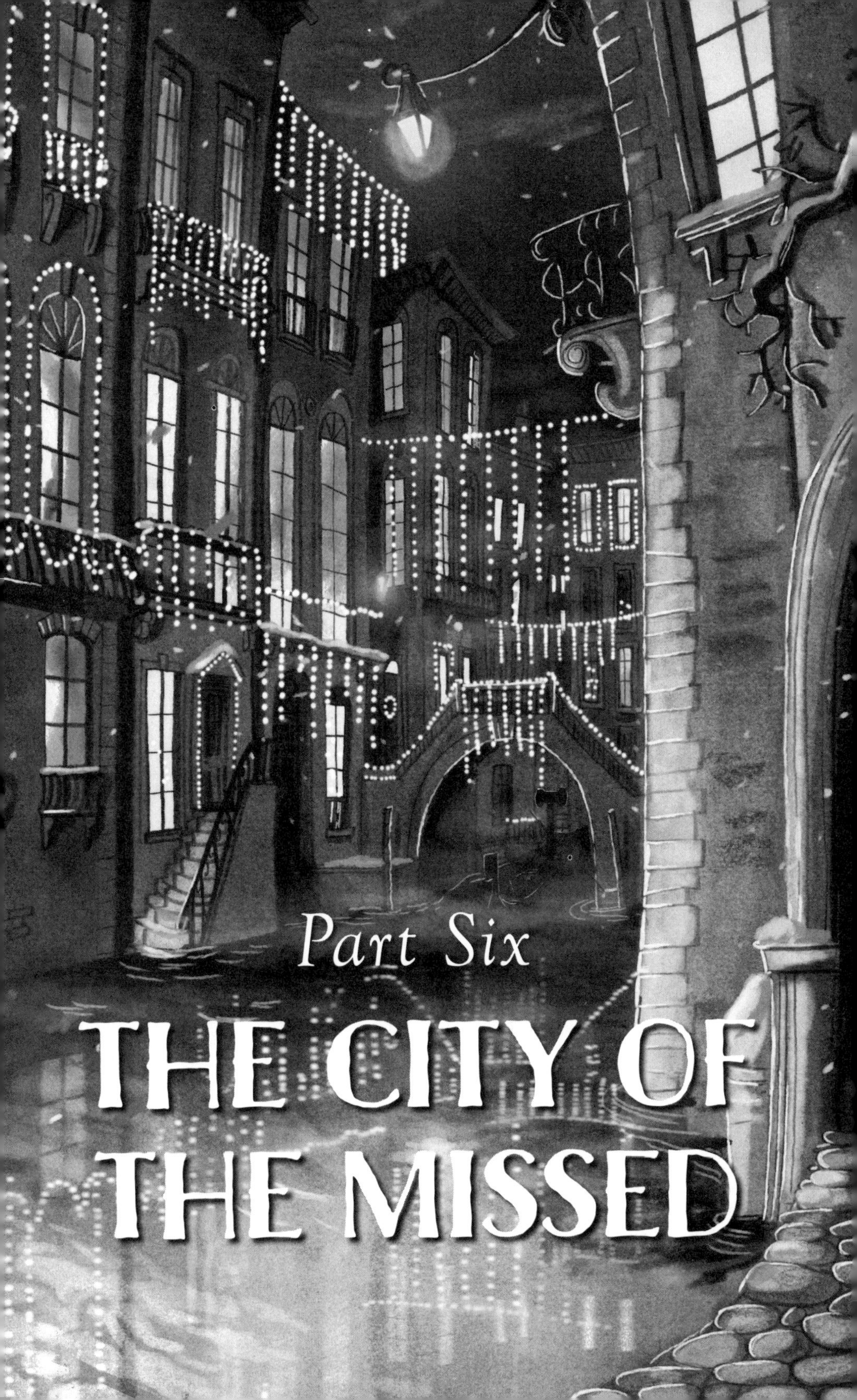

Part Six

THE CITY OF THE MISSED

THE CITY OF THE MISSED

On the other side of the gates were no streets: only a canal bordered by beautiful tall houses with wrought iron balconies. Floating on the water were a number of empty gondolas, which were moored to a striped post sticking up out of the green water. The snow dappled the boats and spotted the water with flakes. The nearest gondola had a dark blue velvet blanket folded on the seat.

"You first!" the Christmas Pig whispered to Jack. "Get in the boat and hide under that blanket!"

Jack did as he was told, lying down in the bottom of the boat and dragging the thick velvet wrap over himself, which had clearly been provided to keep passengers warm. Jack felt the gondola wobble as the Christmas Pig got on board, too, and wriggled under the blanket beside him. They lay curled up together, hoping nobody would notice the lumps in the velvet.

CHAPTER 39

"Blimey," Jack heard one of the Loss Adjusters say.

"Only goes to show," said another voice.

"A dirty little bunny like that, found!" said the third.

"When's the last time you saw a bit of Surplus saved?"

"Not for years and years."

"Well, I've said it before and I'll say it again," came the first voice. "Kids is strange. Imagine that girl liking a muddy lump what had lain in a flower bed for ages!"

A distant whistle pierced the calm.

"Here it comes, bang on time," the voice continued. "Train from Mislaid."

Jack lay very still, curled up beside the Christmas Pig and listening to the sounds of the train chugging nearer and nearer. Soon the noise became deafening. Then, with a loud hiss and a screech of brakes, the train came to a halt. They heard the train doors open, and then the city gates, and then a lot of voices oohing and aahing at the sight of the beautiful gondolas waiting to take them into the heart of the city.

"Welcome, welcome!" the Loss Adjusters cried. "This way, sir . . . Watch your step there, Your Eminence . . . Perhaps you should have a gondola to yourself, Your Highness . . ."

Jack had never heard Loss Adjusters treating lost Things with such respect. Then Jack felt the gondola rock as some Thing climbed inside and adjusted itself on the seat. Strong heat was suddenly beating down on the velvet rug, as though the Thing in the gondola was on fire. Jack couldn't imagine what it might be.

"Would you like this, Your Highness?" came the nutcracker's

voice from just over Jack's head. Jack and the Christmas Pig clutched each other in terror, expecting the velvet wrap to be tweaked off them.

"No, thank you, I never feel the cold," said a lady's voice.

There was a little more creaking of gondolas, and a few more "careful there, Your Worships," and then a Loss Adjuster's voice rang out from what Jack guessed was the gondola at the front.

"Your Highness, Your Eminence, Your Worship, my lords, ladies and gentlemen, welcome to the City of the Missed! Please remain seated for our short journey and then we'll show you to your new homes!"

"We need to think of a way off this boat once we're farther into the city," whispered the Christmas Pig, his snout snuffling against Jack's cheek as the gondola began to move.

"Could we dive off while nobody's looking?" whispered Jack.

"What about this Thing that's sitting in the gondola with us? It's bound to see us and raise the alarm."

"It's very hot, whatever it is," whispered Jack.

"I know," said the Christmas Pig. "It feels like a burning coal. I'm surprised it hasn't set the boat on—"

Without warning, somebody twitched the velvet stole off them. For a horrified moment, Jack couldn't see anything at all, because the gondola was full of a dazzling golden light. It was as though the sun were sitting beside them.

"I'm not a burning coal," said the same lady's voice as before, which came from the very middle of the blazing light. It was so bright that Jack had to close his eyes for a moment, but he could see the Thing, even through his eyelids. "I'm Happiness."

"Happiness?" repeated Jack.

"Yes," she said. "Now do get up and enjoy the view. It's such a beautiful city!"

"We can't sit up," Jack whispered, his eyes watering again as he tried to look at Happiness. "We—we aren't supposed to be here."

"I guessed as much," she said, "but nobody will be able to spot you while you're close to me, because I'm so bright. Do sit up, and we can enjoy the ride together!"

Jack and the Christmas Pig pulled themselves up onto the seat facing Happiness. The heat she was giving off was wonderfully comforting after their hours spent on the snowy wastes, and as long as they didn't look at her directly, they were able to see their surroundings by her light.

The City of the Missed was unlike anything they'd seen so far in the Land of the Lost. The steps of the villas on either side of the canal ran down to the lapping water. It was dusk and strings of silver Christmas lights hung above their heads. From somewhere in the distance came the sound of a choir singing carols. There were many more finding holes over the City of the Missed than there'd been on the Wastes of the Unlamented, and Jack was glad to see them. Once they found DP, they should be able to get back up to the Land of the Living quite easily.

The gondolas passed under a stone bridge, across which a fat silver pocket watch was rolling, its reflection gleaming like a fallen moon. A glittering emerald necklace waved its clasp at the newcomers from an upper window, while a golden sovereign twinkled from a doorway. Jack craned his neck and looked all around, but nowhere could he see any old toys, and no hint of DP. There were, however, other Things, almost as odd and magnificent as Happiness.

"What are they?" Jack asked the Christmas Pig, as a gondola passed, going the other way. It contained a long coil of paper, on which lots of numbers were printed, and a golden throne. These two strange Things were talking to each other in low voices.

"That paper is a lost Fortune," said Happiness, turning to look. "Some rich human Up There has lost all their money. Fortune is talking to a lost Kingdom. A long time ago, a monarch in the Land of the Living lost their throne."

Jack's eyes were getting used to the extreme brightness of Happiness, and he found that if he peeped at her sideways, he could just make out the form of a smiling woman in the middle of the dazzling light.

"How were you lost?" he asked shyly.

"Through carelessness," sighed Happiness. "My owner is an actress. She's charming and talented, but she wasn't as kind as she should have been to the people she cared about, nor as hardworking as she might have been, even though she loved her job. Her gifts once brought her friends and success, but through laziness and selfishness, they slipped away and now, sadly, she has lost me, too."

"How will she get you back again?" asked the Christmas Pig.

"It will be difficult," said Happiness, "because she's looking for me in all the wrong places, and as she isn't used to admitting fault, I'm afraid I may be in the City of the Missed for a long time . . .

perhaps forever. Are you going to tell me what *you're* doing here?" Happiness went on. "Or is it a secret?"

"A secret," said the Christmas Pig, before Jack could answer.

"I thought so. In that case," said Happiness, dropping her voice, "you might want to get out here. We seem to be slowing down, but I'll glow extra bright, so they can't see you."

Jack and the Christmas Pig looked around. Happiness was quite right: the gondolas were definitely slowing down.

"Come on," Jack whispered to the Christmas Pig, bracing himself at the thought of entering the icy water, "we'll go over the side."

"Good luck!" said Happiness.

Jack and the Christmas Pig climbed carefully over the side of the gondola, slipped into the freezing water, and let go of the boat, which drifted away, and Happiness blazing brighter than ever, so that nobody saw them go.

Gasping in the icy cold water, Jack managed to swim over to some steps that led up to the canal bank. However, when he looked back, all he could see of the Christmas Pig was his snout, which was bobbing on the surface. The Christmas Pig was drowning.

FOLLOWED

Jack swam back just in time to stop the pig from sinking forever. By using only one of his arms and kicking his legs hard, Jack succeeded in dragging the waterlogged pig through the water and up the stone steps.

"Thank you, Jack," panted the Christmas Pig, whose toweling body was now greenish from the water. "You're a very good swimmer! I didn't like that at all," he admitted, squeezing himself out so that he stood in a small puddle.

"Why didn't you tell me you couldn't swim?" asked Jack, who was shivering violently now that he was out of the water and standing in the falling snow.

"I didn't know I couldn't swim until I was already sinking," said the Christmas Pig, "and then the water was in my mouth, so I couldn't tell you." After wringing out his ears, which left them somewhat lopsided, the Christmas Pig said, "Come on. Let's find DP."

One good thing about going in the canal was that the Christmas Pig's tummy beans weren't making as much noise as usual, because they were stuck together. He and Jack set off through the narrow streets of the City of the Missed.

Cobbled and lined with gorgeous villas, the alleys were just as beautiful as the waterways. Sparkling Christmas wreaths hung on doors and candlelit Christmas trees glowed in the windows. Jack and the Christmas Pig passed a few Things as they crossed snow-covered squares in the gathering darkness, but none of them seemed very curious about Jack and the Christmas Pig. A magnificent diamond brooch in the shape of a unicorn bowed politely as he made his way into his villa, and a beautiful, gold-embossed book flicked her pages in a casual wave as she passed, but just as in Bother-It's-Gone, Jack was troubled by the lack of toys.

"D'you think they put cuddly animals in a different part of town?" he asked the Christmas Pig.

"Maybe," said the Christmas Pig. "This does seem a larger city than the others. I think we're getting nearer the place where they're singing carols, though . . ."

"Yes," said Jack, who was still shivering from his icy dip in the canal. "D'you think it's a party?"

"Perhaps," said the Christmas Pig. He squinted over his shoulder, looked as though he was going to say something, but seemed to change his mind. "Come on, let's see if we can find out where the toys are."

They walked on, but the farther they went, the stronger Jack's feeling that they weren't alone became. Twice he glanced back and saw nothing, but on the third occasion he thought he caught a glimpse of something black whisking away around a corner out of sight.

“CP, did you see that?” Jack whispered.

“Yes,” said the Christmas Pig, who’d looked back at the same moment as Jack. “I *thought* something was following us. I think we might be safer mingling in a crowd . . . let’s head for the singers. Come on, quick.”

THE PERFORMERS

They hurried on toward the place where the carols were being sung, and after a few minutes, they found themselves standing in an archway that looked out onto a large and beautiful square, strung with gleaming silver Christmas lights just like the canals. A choir of instruments was singing in one corner of the square. All of them—from the French horns and the violins, to the flutes and the tubas—had human voices now, and Jack had never heard carols sung so beautifully. For just a few seconds, he forgot how cold he was in his sodden pajamas, and simply marveled at the wonderful sights and sounds.

The square lay in front of a huge white palace, which had a golden roof and arched windows. On either side of the palace doors stood two Loss Adjusters, a pencil sharpener and a mallet, who, like the Loss Adjusters guarding the city gates, wore black hats with long black plumes.

A balcony stretched the length of the palace and Jack could see people-shaped Things standing there, listening to the choir of instruments. Like Happiness, each of these Things was giving off light. One was scarlet, another green, and several were bright blue. Jack was too far away to be able to see what the figures in the middle of the colored lights looked like, but he knew they must be extremely important, to live in the golden-roofed palace.

Meanwhile, right ahead of where Jack and the Christmas Pig stood, was a crowd of other Things packed together in the falling snow, their shadows long in the light of the dying day. They seemed to be watching some kind of performance that was taking place in their middle.

"Let's hide in that crowd," whispered the Christmas Pig, glancing over his shoulder again. "Keep your eyes peeled for DP!"

So they set off into the square, Jack's bare, frozen feet leaving footprints and the Christmas Pig's trotters leaving round, damp spots in the snow, and neither of them noticed the figure cloaked in black that slid out from behind a marble column to follow them.

None of the Things in the crowd took much notice of Jack and the Christmas Pig as they sidled in among them. When at last they were able to see what the crowd was watching, Jack and the Christmas Pig also stopped and stared.

All the performers were transparent and human-shaped, just like Pretense. A jester was juggling and doing backflips, while a little man with a long mustache was spinning plates on long poles. A chef was flipping pancakes, catching them every time, while a ballerina twirled in endless pirouettes. One old man was tying a long length of rope into complicated knots, and another was performing card tricks.

"What are they?" Jack wondered aloud to a brand-new smartphone standing beside him.

"Lost Knacks," said the phone. "Clever little tricks that humans can do but which, through age or injury, poor memory or lack of practice, they lose."

"Can't they get them back?" asked Jack.

"Sometimes," said the phone. "Yesterday, a very clever magic trick was whooshed back up to the Land of the Living while we were watching. Very disappointing, because he hadn't finished. We're always sorry to lose Knacks, because they put on a show for us this time every evening—but the Knacks are just the warm-up act. Wait until you see today's Talent!"

Sure enough, the Lost Knacks finally bowed to much cheering, and they ran, tumbled, bounced, and pirouetted out of the square and out of sight.

Now a very large transparent lady, who was wearing a jeweled dress, strode into the middle of the square. Some of the onlookers cheered, but the phone groaned.

"You're out of luck. I was hoping for one of our Stories—they're always very entertaining—but it's a Voice."

Voice took a deep breath and began to sing in a language Jack didn't understand. Her song echoed off the stone arches and palace wall, making Jack's ears ring. He supposed Voice must be very talented, judging by the way all the jewelry and fine books were sighing in admiration, but the phone leaned over to Jack and said,

"She was lost by an opera singer, Up There. I'm not much of a one for opera. Think I'll be getting home."

Phone hopped away. Jack would have liked to follow, because Voice's song was making his ears ring, but at that moment a Thing whispered in his ear. "Excuse me. Are you the ones who're looking for a toy pig?"

THE KING'S INVITATION

Jack spun around to face a figure that appeared to be that of a woman. A black cloak hid her from head to toe, though violet light escaped from the hood and beneath the hem. Noticing that Jack had turned round, the Christmas Pig did so, too, and when he saw the cloaked figure, he took his trotters away from his ears and grasped Jack's arm, ready to run.

"Don't be alarmed," said the female voice from beneath the cloak. "I was sent to fetch you by one who means you well."

"Was it Happiness?" asked Jack.

"Yes, Happiness," said the woman, "but unless you want to get her into trouble, keep that quiet. A Thing could get eaten for helping you two. You've caused a lot of trouble. Follow me, and I'll explain."

The Christmas Pig still looked suspicious, but they followed the figure away from Voice and the crowd, into the shadows beneath an archway. Here the mysterious figure threw back her hood. She glowed with violet light as Happiness had shone with gold, but gave off no heat. Her face looked older than that of Happiness, and rather less kind.

"D'you know where DP is?" asked Jack.

"I'm afraid not," said the woman, "but the king does. His Majesty invites you both to dinner at the palace, where all will be explained."

"What king is this?" asked the Christmas Pig suspiciously. "The Loser's in charge down here. Everyone knows that."

"The Loser is in overall command," said the violet lady, "but we have a royal family here in the City of the Missed. I am His Majesty's ambassador. If you really want to find your pig, the king is the only one who can help . . . I'd have thought you'd be glad of some shelter, at least," she added, because Jack's teeth were chattering and green water was still oozing out of the Christmas Pig.

"It would be nice to get warm," Jack admitted, but the Christmas Pig still looked suspicious.

"Would you excuse us for a moment?" he said to the violet lady.

"Certainly," she replied, though she didn't seem pleased.

"I know she doesn't seem very friendly, but she must be good, if Happiness sent her," Jack muttered into the Christmas Pig's ear, once they'd moved a short distance away. He had trouble making himself heard, because Voice was still echoing around the square, but at least that meant the violet lady couldn't eavesdrop. "DP might be inside the palace! I love him so much, they might have let him live there! Perhaps he's become royal!"

CHAPTER 42

"I don't believe it," said the Christmas Pig, whose damp snout was slowly freezing in the evening air. "I never heard there was any king down here except the Loser. And how does that lady know who we're looking for? We never told Happiness we were after DP!"

"I expect word's got round," said Jack. "I asked Sheriff Specs and the chess piece about him."

"I still don't like it," said the pig. "It smells like a trap to me."

"This is the first time anybody's told us they know where DP is!" said Jack, now starting to get angry. "You heard what Poem said! We've got to succeed before Christmas Day, or I'll be trapped and I'll never be able to take DP home! There can't be much time left!"

When the Christmas Pig didn't answer, Jack said, "Fine, don't come—but I'm going!"

And with that, Jack turned and strode back toward the violet lady, who stood burning in the shadowy archway like a purple flame. Jack heard the Christmas Pig's belly beans behind him, and knew he was following.

THE PALACE

The violet lady accepted the news that they were ready to follow her with a brief smile, which showed her rather pointed teeth, then led them toward the palace, her black cloak flying behind her in the breeze.

"How are we going to get past the Loss Adjusters?" asked Jack as they approached the golden palace doors.

"Oh, you needn't worry about them," said the violet lady, with a haughty smile. "The king's in charge of the Loss Adjusters here in the City of the Missed, and I'm His Majesty's representative. Good evening to you!" she said grandly to the pencil sharpener and the mallet, who both bowed as each opened a door. The mallet's head was so heavy he nearly toppled over, but saved himself by clutching the door handle.

"Good evening, Your Excellency," they said together.

A wonderful warmth enveloped Jack and the Christmas Pig as they stepped over the threshold of the palace. They now stood on a thick crimson carpet which was soft under Jack's bruised, frozen feet. Twin fires burned beneath two marble fireplaces on either side of a magnificent staircase with golden bannisters. At the foot of the stairs stood the very same diamond earrings Jack had seen back in Mislaid. They seemed to be employed now as maids, because they took the violet lady's black cloak, bowed, then wriggled away, disappearing through a side door.

"This way," said the violet lady to Jack and the Christmas Pig as she started to climb the stairs.

"May we ask your name, Your Excellency?" said the Christmas Pig as they followed, repeating the title he'd heard the Loss Adjusters use. Now that she was unrobed, their companion filled the hall with her violet light. A tall, thin woman, she looked down at them as she said, "My name is Ambition."

"How does someone lose their ambition?" wondered Jack out loud.

"By being a fool," said Ambition coldly. "My mistress and I achieved great things together. She's a politician—or rather, she was. She suffered a small setback—lost a trifling vote—but that oughtn't to have mattered!" cried Ambition, coming to a sudden halt, so that Jack nearly walked into her. Her eyes emitted sparks, and for a moment, Jack found her rather frightening.

"We could have recovered from that setback and climbed together to even greater heights! But no . . . she lost me, the weak-willed fool!" shouted Ambition, shaking her fist at the finding hole in the ceiling.

The sound of her words echoing off the marble walls seemed to bring Ambition back to herself. She took several deep breaths. "My apologies," she said stiffly. "I've lived here in the palace for several years now, waiting for her to find me again. Sometimes I fear it will never happen . . . but none of this will help you find your pig."

She began to climb the stairs again. Jack and the Christmas Pig glanced at each other, then followed. Jack could tell the Christmas Pig was having even more doubts about Ambition now, and in truth, she'd made Jack quite nervous, too. However, he didn't want to turn back, so he tried to look cheerful and unconcerned.

At the top of the stairs, they found more double doors, which were opened by a pair of solid gold fish knives.

"Your Excellency," they muttered respectfully as Ambition passed through into the room beyond. Jack and the Christmas Pig followed, watched curiously by the glinting knives.

THE ROYAL FAMILY

The room they now entered was even grander than the hall, with gilded columns and mirrors. The vaulted ceiling was painted with pictures of the three cities of the Land of the Lost: the low wooden houses of Disposable, the neat snow-topped chalets of Bother-It's-Gone, and the villas and canals of the City of the Missed. Beneath the painted ceiling stood a long candlelit table, which was laid with enough golden plates and crystal glasses for fifteen Things. At the head of the table stood a large golden throne, which was currently empty.

In front of another fire, in a ball of emerald light, stood a very handsome young man who was examining himself in the mirror over the mantelpiece. He looked delighted with what he saw there.

"Good evening," he said, without taking his eyes off his own reflection, but turning his head this way and that, to get a better view of his profile.

"That's Beauty," said Ambition, indicating the green man, "and that," she said, pointing to a ball of orange light, inside which stood a young man with a plump, smiley face, "is Optimism. They'll entertain you while I tell His Majesty his guests have arrived."

Ambition swept out of the room, leaving Jack and the Christmas Pig feeling nervous and extremely shabby in all this splendor. However, the moment the golden fish knives had closed the door behind Ambition, Optimism came bounding over to Jack and the Christmas Pig, beaming from ear to ear. He had round, innocent eyes and, like Happiness, gave off a pleasant warmth. After seizing Jack's hand and shaking it, and doing the same with the Christmas Pig's trotter, he cried, "Marvelous to meet you! What jolly good Things you are! I feel as though I've known you forever! Let's be best friends!"

"Hello," said Jack timidly.

"I hear you're looking for an old toy pig?" said Optimism, bouncing excitedly on the balls of his feet.

"Yes," said Jack.

"Well, I'm *sure* you'll find him! Everything will work out splendidly! And you'll love our king! He's a very good Thing"—for just a second, Optimism's smile faltered, but then he beamed as widely as ever—"deep down, you know!"

"Isn't *anybody* going to admire me?" asked Beauty indignantly, turning from the mirror to look at Jack and the Christmas Pig.

"Oh—er—yes," said the Christmas Pig. "You're very handsome."

"Which is more than can be said for you two," said Beauty with a smirk, looking from the now-bedraggled Christmas Pig, with his lopsided ears, to Jack's filthy bare feet and muddy pajamas. "*Your* beauty must be here somewhere, too! Or perhaps you never had any to lose?"

With this rude remark, he turned back to the mirror. Then a door opened at the far end of the room. A ball of indigo light entered. For a moment, Jack thought it might be the king, but as the light came nearer, he saw a very old lady shuffling along in its center.

"Good evening," she said in a high, cracked voice.

"Good evening," said the Christmas Pig.

"This is Memory," said Optimism.

Memory peered at the Christmas Pig for a moment or two, then said, "Eighty-five years ago, my mistress owned a pig, but hers was of china; what we call a piggy bank. Its sides were painted with little blue flowers and she used to keep her pocket money inside it. One Sunday afternoon, eighty-four years ago, my mistress's younger sister, Amelia Louise—"

"Memory," said Beauty with a yawn, "nobody's interested. Nobody cares."

"Oh, I'm sure it will be a smashing story!" said Optimism, still beaming. Jack wondered how he could smile so much without his face hurting.

"—broke that piggy bank with the little blue flowers—"

"We've heard this at least a thousand times already," groaned Beauty, while Memory continued to mumble.

The door at the far end of the room opened again. Six balls of glowing blue light entered the room, each of which had an identical man inside it, all of them small and neat and serious looking. They couldn't *all* be the king, Jack thought, getting more confused by the second.

"Good evening," said the six blue men, speaking with one voice, and drowning out Memory, who continued to mumble her story about the piggy bank. "We are the Principles."

They bowed in unison and Jack, who didn't know what else to do, bowed back, as did the Christmas Pig, whose tummy beans, now drying out in the heat from the fire, made a crunching noise.

"I thought the king told you to stay in your rooms?" asked Beauty, frowning at the Principles' reflections in the mirror.

"After carefully considering His Majesty's order," said the Principles, speaking together as before, "we decided it would be against ourselves to stay in our rooms."

Jack whispered to the Christmas Pig, "What are Principles?"

The Principles seemed to have heard him, because they answered together, "We are the Things who make humans behave with honesty and decency. Alas, our owner—a businessman—lost us one by one in pursuit of riches. He is now a wealthy crook. He likes the money, yet he is unhappy, because he knows he was better loved and respected while he still had us. Unfortunately, lost Principles are among the hardest Things to find, so we expect to live here forever. We have therefore taken on a new job. We attempt to keep the king on the path of righteousness."

"And does the king often need your help?" asked the Christmas Pig.

But before the Principles could answer, there was a loud fanfare and the doors behind them opened.

THE KING

The whole dining room now filled with scarlet light, which glinted off the crystal goblets and turned the plates bloodred. The crimson figure standing in the doorway made even Ambition, who'd entered the room behind him, seem dim by comparison.

Beauty, Optimism, and the Principles bowed, and Jack and the Christmas Pig copied them, while Memory dropped into a deep curtsy and fell silent at last.

"This," said Ambition proudly to Jack and the Christmas Pig, "is Power, our king. Your Majesty, these are the two you've been waiting for: the ones who're looking for the lost pig."

By screwing up his eyes, Jack was able to make out the figure casting the scarlet light. He was a big, fierce-looking man with a sour expression and a jutting jaw.

"Welcome," he said, in a booming voice. "What d'you think of my city? Do you like it?"

"It's very beautiful, Your Majesty," said the Christmas Pig. Jack was too frightened to speak.

"Beautiful?" said Power, who seemed displeased. "Many places are beautiful. I consider my city to be magnificent. Stupendous. *SUBLIME!*"

He thundered the last word and everyone jumped.

"It's those things, too!" squeaked the Christmas Pig.

Power turned to the Principles.

"I *THOUGHT*," he shouted, "I told you to stay in your *ROOMS?*"

"It was against ourselves to stay in our rooms," repeated the Principles, speaking in one voice as before.

Power's huge hands balled themselves into fists and he ground his teeth. Jack and the Christmas Pig both took a step backward.

"Your Majesty," murmured Ambition, laying a hand on Power's thick arm. "I beg you to remember our objective."

Her touch seemed to make Power think better of shouting at the Principles.

"You're quite right, Ambition. Everyone, sit *DOWN!*" boomed the king, and he strolled to the head of the table and took his place on the throne.

Jack sat down between the Christmas Pig and Beauty, who was now admiring himself in the back of a shining spoon. Optimism settled into the seat opposite Jack, smiling as widely as ever.

"There's no need to be nervous!" he called across the table. "I just know everything will turn out wonderfully!"

"Excellent," growled Power, in response to something Ambition had just whispered in his ear. Even his ordinary speaking voice was so loud that it made the cutlery rattle. "And the door's locked?"

"It will be, after the servants confirm she's gone to bed," said Ambition. "As for the other . . . well, I'm afraid I haven't been able to find her. Your Majesty knows how she's always flitting off into dirty corners where no decent Thing would go. I had the Loss Adjusters try and hunt her d—I mean, find her," she corrected herself, with half a glance at Jack, "but alas, they were unsuccessful."

Jack gathered that Power and Ambition were talking about the Things who ought to have been sitting in the two empty spaces left at the table, but he felt too scared to ask questions.

Power now clapped his enormous hands together twice. At once, a procession of Things came hurrying through the servants' door, all carrying food, and a very odd assortment it was, too.

There was a single peppermint as large as Jack's head, a few giant crisps, a pillow-like slice of birthday cake, pieces of popcorn the size of cauliflowers, and largest of all, a chocolate tree decoration wrapped in colored foil and shaped like a fat Santa Claus. The sugar tongs carrying it groaned as she heaved it onto the table.

"The only food here is lost food, of course," boomed the king down the table at Jack, as the Things that had delivered the food ran out of the room again. "We Things have no need of food—but *YOU* will want to eat," he said, glaring at Jack, "because *YOU*, of course, are a *LIVING BOY*!"

POWER'S PLAN

As soon as Power shouted the words "living boy," loud metallic clicks sounded from either end of the room and Jack realized that the servants outside had just locked the doors.

"We were afraid of something like this," muttered the Principles all together.

"He isn't a living boy," said the Christmas Pig in a squeaky voice. "He's an action figure!"

"That's right," said Jack, whose mouth had gone dry. "Pajama Boy, with the power of sleep and dreams."

"He's got his own cartoon!" said the Christmas Pig.

"We disapprove of lying," said the Principles in one voice.

"Eighty years ago," piped up Memory, "my mistress's sister, Amelia Louise, was caught lying when—"

"*QUIET!*" yelled Power, banging his huge fist on the table. One of the crystal goblets toppled over and cracked. Memory fell silent again. Power got to his feet, burning a deeper, darker red than ever, and all the Things around the table looked nervous except for Ambition, from whose eyes sparks were flying again, and whose pointed teeth were revealed in a wide grin.

"Do you *KNOW*," thundered Power, staring at Jack, "why I'm *HERE*, in the Land of the Lost?"

"No," whispered Jack.

Beneath the table, the Christmas Pig stretched out a trotter to hold Jack's hand.

"My owner," said Power, beginning to pace up and down, "lost me by failing to stamp down hard enough"—he smacked one huge fist into the other hand—"on his *ENEMIES*!

"Together, we ruled an entire *COUNTRY*! To keep me, my master kept the *PEOPLE*"—as Power bawled this word, he screwed up his face in disgust and hatred—"in their proper places, which is to say, *ON THEIR KNEES*!" he thundered, a mad look in his bright red eyes. "But *THEN*," he bellowed, "a boy like *YOU* dared *CHALLENGE* my master in *PUBLIC*! And *THAT CHILD*," shouted Power, "gave the *PEOPLE* courage to *REVOLT*!"

Power's voice rose to a scream.

"AND I WAS SUCKED DOWN HERE, TO THE LAND OF THE LOST!"

"Power, dear," said Beauty, "*do* stop shouting. Quite apart from the racket, it makes you look awfully ugly."

"So you've lured us here to take revenge on living boys, have you?" asked the Christmas Pig, still gripping Jack's hand under the table.

"Of course not!" sneered Ambition. "We aren't interested in

petty revenge! Our aim is to do whatever we must to rise higher, to gain more prestige, to achieve greater success—"

"To increase our *POWER!*" roared the king. "We know what you seek: the one called DP—"

"Where is he?" asked Jack desperately. "Do you know?"

"YES, I KNOW!" screamed Power. *"BUT YOU WILL NEVER FIND HIM, NEVER, BECAUSE I AM ABOUT TO TRADE YOU TO THE LOSER! IN RETURN, HE WILL REWARD ME, AND WITH AMBITION AS MY QUEEN, I SHALL RULE STILL VASTER TERRITORIES, UNTIL MY POWER RIVALS HIS OWN!"*

"Calmly, Your Majesty, calmly," said Ambition, laying a bony hand on Power's arm again. "We need votes to proceed, remember . . . Now listen, all of you," she said, addressing Beauty, Optimism, Memory, and the Principles. "If we trade these two to the Loser, he might give us things in return. Perhaps an enlarged palace, with even more mirrors"—she glanced at Beauty—"or a guarantee he'll stay outside the city walls! We might even be allowed a say in who comes to the City of the Missed! Occasionally some Thing arrives that is not of the standard we expect . . . you all remember that scruffy Poem, I'm sure, and that ghastly, common Pretense . . . Beauty, how do you vote?"

"You know, I'm awfully afraid this is going to turn into a fight," said Beauty, getting to his feet. "And I *never* fight. One's hair gets messed up and in severe cases, one's teeth may be knocked out. I shall go to bed. Vote without me."

"You'll go nowhere," snarled Power. "The doors are locked.

Vote, or *I'll* knock out your teeth. Do you want to hand them to the Loser, yes or no?"

"Oh, well, if it means more mirrors, yes," sighed Beauty, sitting back down again. He picked up his spoon and fell back to admiring his reflection.

"Memory, dear," said Ambition, "you agree, I'm sure, that we should hand these fugitives to the Loser?"

"Sixty-nine years ago," said Memory, in her high, cracked voice, "my mistress and her sister, Amelia Louise, went to see a movie called *The Fugitive*—"

"Memory, concentrate," snapped Ambition. "We're taking a vote. Should we hand the boy and the pig to the Loser, yes or no?"

The old lady glowing with indigo light turned her gaze upon Jack and the Christmas Pig. There was a long silence. Then Memory said, "No. *They* don't stop me remembering things. I like them."

"Thank you, Memory," whispered the Christmas Pig, still clutching Jack's hand under the table.

"And you, Optimism?" demanded Power.

"I told them everything would work out wonderfully!" said Optimism, his lip wobbling. "I told them you were good and kind, Power!"

"*VOTE!*" thundered Power.

"Well, I vote no," said Optimism, with a little sob. "And I'm sure that deep down, Power—deep, deep down—there's a little bit of good in you, and when you've thought it over, you'll change your mind and let them live in the palace with us!"

"*SHUT UP!*" roared Power. "What about you, Principles? You

realize these two have broken the laws of the Land of the Lost? It is forbidden for the living to enter here!"

"True," said the Principles, speaking all together as usual. "We disapprove of breaking the law."

"Then you vote yes?" asked Ambition eagerly, but before the Principles could answer, there came another couple of metallic clicks, and a familiar voice spoke from the end of the room.

"Why was I locked in my room?"

A blaze of golden light filled the dining hall, as Happiness entered.

THE LAST TWO GUESTS

I—I thought you needed a rest after your long journey, Your Highness," said Ambition nervously, dropping into a curtsy as Happiness moved into the room, shedding golden light all around her. "I didn't think you'd want to be bothered with this tedious bit of business, the very evening you arrived."

"How did you get *OUT*?" demanded Power. "Come to that—how did you get through *THOSE* doors?"

"*I* unlocked them," said a second voice. "You know very well that no lock can contain me, Power."

Jack hadn't noticed the second Thing that had entered the room, because Happiness's radiance had blinded him for a moment, but now he saw a woman as tall as Ambition, though far more strongly built. She was very beautiful, but the soft pink light she gave off was less bright than that of the other Things. Unlike her fellow royals, she had wings: not stiff, upstanding wings of golden plastic, like those of Broken Angel back on the Wastes, but vast feathery wings of white shading to deep pink, which trailed behind her on the floor like a train.

"How lovely to see you two again," said Happiness, smiling at Jack and the Christmas Pig. "This," she said, indicating her companion, "is my friend Hope."

The pink lady also smiled at Jack and the Christmas Pig and terrified as they were, they smiled back. Hope and Happiness sat down in the last two chairs at the table.

"We hear you're taking a vote on handing our guests to the Loser," said Happiness. "Please continue. We'd be glad to take part."

"Very well," said Ambition. "This living boy and his pig have broken the law in pursuit of an impossible goal. The only way for a lost Thing to return to the Land of the Living is by being found Up There, and as DP can *never* be found Up There—"

"Why can't he?" said Jack.

"Because a lorry ran over him on the motorway," said Ambition, with a cruel smile. "All that remains of your DP up in the Land of the Living are a few scattered beans and a bit of fluff. He cannot be found, so he remains with us, forever."

"No," whispered Jack, "I don't believe it. It can't be true."

But as he said it, he remembered the tiny shake of his head Grandpa had given Gran, when he came back to the car after looking for DP.

"You *can* still get him back," said the Christmas Pig fiercely, still clutching Jack's hand beneath the table. "I promise, Jack, you can save DP."

"Well spoken, Pig," said Hope. "Ambition has forgotten what night it is, up in the Land of the Living." Turning to the king, she went on, "These two came bravely into the Land of the Lost in the hope of achieving the impossible and tonight, the night for miracles and lost causes, they have a chance."

"Which they richly deserve," said Happiness. "I vote against giving them to the Loser."

"As do I," said Hope.

"Then," said Ambition, placing her hand again on Power's arm, because the king looked as though he was about to explode with rage again, "we have three votes for giving them to the Loser and four against. The deciding votes lie with the Principles."

She turned back to the six identical small blue men.

"You agree that these two have broken the law?"

"We do," said the Principles, speaking in one voice, as always.

"But handing a living boy to the Loser would be murder and that's the worst crime there is!" said the Christmas Pig.

"Also true," said the Principles, together.

"I only want DP back!" said Jack desperately. "I never wanted to do any harm!"

"How do you vote, Principles?" Ambition demanded, ignoring Jack. "What should happen to liars and rule breakers, who seek to disobey the ancient law of the Land of the Lost? No matter their motive, don't you agree that they belong to the Loser, to punish as he sees fit?"

"Yes," said three of the Principles, but the rest answered, "No."

"Seven-six—we won!" Jack whispered to the Christmas Pig, but at that moment, Power jumped to his feet.

"I VOTE THAT THE VOTES DON'T COUNT!" he roared, smacking the giant peppermint to the floor, his teeth bared and his fists clenched. Beauty sank slowly beneath the table and out of sight, taking his shining spoon with him. Memory began to mumble something about Amelia Louise, but nobody heard what it was, because Power now shouted, *"LOSS ADJUSTERS! TAKE THESE THINGS TO THE LOSER!"*

FLIGHT

At these words, both sets of doors at either end of the room burst open, and with a great clamor and clatter, in ran the biggest group of Loss Adjusters Jack had seen since Mislaid. There were razors, scissors, pincers, and knives; wire clippers, chisels, and the huge mallet, all of them wearing the plumed black hats of the palace guards. Jack and the Christmas Pig both jumped up from their chairs. Jack grabbed some popcorn, ready to throw it, and the Christmas Pig picked up the giant peppermint.

"*SEIZE THEM!*" roared Power, and for a moment Jack was certain that they were going to be captured and taken to the Loser's Lair, and that he'd never see Mum or DP again.

But then, to his amazement, Jack felt a warm, strong arm encircle him, heard a great whoosh of wings, and felt himself rising into the air, up above the roar and clash of all the metal Things below. Hope had caught Jack up in one arm and the Christmas Pig in the other, and she now flew on her huge wings across the room, while Power screamed in rage. Happiness increased her own dazzling light, confusing the Things giving chase, and Hope flew through the double doors at the end of the room and off along a dark corridor.

"Where are we going?" asked Jack, clutching Hope's strong arm as they flew, while the Loss Adjusters clattered along in pursuit.

"To DP," said Hope. "I'm not allowed to enter the place where he lives: only the most precious in the Land of the Lost may set foot there. I can carry you most of the way, but you'll have to do the last bit yourself. Grab that tapestry off the wall!" she added, and Jack reached out and tugged it. The heavy material broke free and billowed behind them. It was so heavy it took all Jack's strength to keep hold of it, and it slowed their progress a little. Jack could hear the shouts and the bangs of the Loss Adjusters, and thought they seemed to be gaining ground, but Hope flew up a spiral staircase, the tapestry trailing in their wake, until they reached a locked and bolted door.

Jack was sure they were trapped, but as Hope soared toward it, the bolt flew back and the door crashed open, and they flew outside into the falling snow.

"Quickly," said Hope, landing on the golden palace roof and setting Jack and the Christmas Pig down. "Wrap that tapestry around yourselves so I can carry you easily. The journey will be cold and you're already damp."

Jack and the Christmas Pig wrapped the heavy tapestry around themselves, Hope unfurled her powerful wings again, seized hold of the material, and rose once more into the air, now carrying them below her in a kind of hammock.

Through the thick tapestry Jack could hear the screams of rage of the Loss Adjusters who'd raced out onto the roof behind them, and Power's shout of "*COME BACK! BRING THEM BACK!*"

But Hope kept flying, and soon the sound of shouting grew distant, then died away completely. Now the only sound they could hear was the beating of Hope's wide, strong wings.

49

THE STORY OF HOPE

Though dusty, it was cozy inside the tapestry, because Jack and the Christmas Pig were snuggled up together. After their scary dash through Power's palace, Jack found it comforting to feel the Christmas Pig's trotters around him. He didn't even mind the smell of dank canal water the Christmas Pig was giving off.

Only now they were safe did Jack fully realize that he was on his way to DP at last, and in his excitement he gave the Christmas Pig a squeeze.

"We've nearly done it!" he said. "I was so scared back there, weren't you?"

"Very scared," said the Christmas Pig. "We should thank Hope. Without her, we'd be on the way to the Loser's Lair right now."

"I know," said Jack, and raising his voice he said, "thank you very much, Hope!"

"You're welcome," came her voice from above them. "Are you comfortable?"

"Very," said Jack.

"We aren't too heavy for you, are we?" asked the Christmas Pig.

"Oh no," said Hope. "I've carried far heavier than you."

"How were you lost, Hope?" asked Jack.

"That's a sad story, I'm afraid," came Hope's voice, over the beating of her wings. "My owner is in prison."

"Prison?" gasped Jack. "What did they do?"

"Nothing wrong," said Hope. "On the contrary, she was doing a good thing: protesting against a ruler very like Power. The ruler was furious, so he locked her up, pretending she'd broken the law. The judge was too scared to rule against the president, so my owner is currently in a cell with ten others, where there isn't enough to eat and barely room to lie down."

"That's terrible!" said Jack.

"It is," agreed Hope. "At this moment, she can't see how things will ever get better for her, because they've told her she'll be in prison for twenty years. She lost me when she heard the length of her sentence, but she'll find me again, and sooner than she thinks."

"How do you know?" asked Jack.

"She has a wonderful family and many friends outside the prison walls," said Hope. "When she realizes that they're working hard to free her, she'll find me again and I'll help her bear her situation, dreadful though it is. I may not shine as brightly as my friend Happiness, but my flame is harder to extinguish."

Jack and the Christmas Pig swayed gently back and forth in the

tapestry as Hope bore them onward. Jack was starting to feel very sleepy. After a while, he thought he heard a new sound, like the breathing of some huge slumbering beast, and he smelled something vaguely familiar. By shifting his position a little, he was able to peek over the edge of the tapestry. Far below, he saw the ocean, which was as dark as the night sky above. Snow was still falling, and Jack could see Hope's wide, pale wings reflected in the waves.

"Where are we going, Hope?" Jack asked.

"To the Island of the Beloved," said Hope. "Only a few Things on the mainland know it exists. The truly loved are never moved off the island, so the Things in the cities never meet them. But I know the island's there, because I've flown over it.

"You should sleep now, because we've got a long way to travel. I'll wake you when it's time for you to go on alone. You've done very well, you'll complete your mission before Christmas Day! I should think you'll be home at least an hour before midnight!"

So Jack wriggled back down inside the tapestry, closed his eyes, and allowed his face to press up against the Christmas Pig's. "All those lies Ambition told us, about me not being able to get DP back!" he muttered into the Christmas Pig's damp ear. "I want to thank you, too, CP. I'd never have been able to get DP back without you."

"That's all right," said the Christmas Pig, in a strangely muffled voice. "Sleep now. You heard Hope. We've still got a long way to go."

Jack closed his eyes, squeezed the Christmas Pig again, felt the familiar belly beans, and breathed in his satisfying, grubby smell. Soon Jack was on the verge of sleep, and on his lips he tasted a salty wetness, and knew he must be dreaming of the sea, far, far below.

Part Seven

THE ISLAND OF THE BELOVED

50 THE ISLAND OF THE BELOVED

Many hours later, Jack was woken by Hope's voice calling him. "Jack, it's time," she said. "Get ready. I'm afraid you're going to get wet, but I can take you no farther!"

Jack could barely open his eyes, because the light pouring in through either end of the tapestry was as blinding as that of Happiness. The tapestry itself had become hot, and his pajamas were warm and dry again. Even his feet were warm. He realized they'd come to a place where the sun was shining brightly.

"Ready?" called Hope. "Wriggle out with your feet first: it's not a long drop, I've flown as low as I dare!"

"Come on, CP!" said Jack.

"You first," said the Christmas Pig, and Jack, who guessed he was worried about jumping into the sea as he couldn't swim, said, "I'll be there when you hit the water, CP, don't worry!"

Jack wriggled down the tapestry hammock. The smell of the

sea was stronger than ever now, and he could feel the heat of the sun on his bare feet. Taking a deep breath, he pushed himself out of the tapestry.

As Hope had promised, the drop was short, and seconds later, he found himself knee-deep in the crystal clear sea, which was as warm as a bath. Looking around, he saw a beautiful island with swaying palm trees and soft white sand. The cloudless sky was periwinkle blue and dotted with many finding holes and there, running down the beach toward him, ahead of a multitude of other old toys who'd rushed to see what was going on, was DP.

"DP!" shouted Jack, starting to laugh and cry at the same time. "DP, it's me!"

DP looked exactly as he always had: gray, wonky-eared, and button-eyed, and he was beaming as he ran down the beach and into the sea. Jack splashed through the water, his arms wide open, and DP's button eyes were leaking tears, and then they reached each other and hugged as tightly as ever a boy and his toy hugged, and Jack breathed in DP's smell of bed, and garden, and of the trace of Mum's perfume, from where she kissed DP good night.

"DP, I found you, I found you!" sobbed Jack, and behind the old pig a hundred battered old toys cheered and clapped their hands, their paws, and their hooves, and one little puffin turned a somersault. "Everything's all right again! Holly threw you and I was so angry and I knew you were alone on the motorway and I couldn't stand it and I yelled and smashed up my room—"

"I know, Jack, I know," said DP, patting Jack on his back. "But it's all right, now. You've found me! Come into my house!"

With his worn old trotter around Jack's shoulders, DP guided him out of the sea onto the beach, while all the beloved Things watching continued to cheer.

"I live there," said DP, pointing to a little yellow beach house, "with somebody you know."

To Jack's amazement, he saw the old toilet roll angel peering out of the window, a wide smile on his bearded face.

The beach house was light, bright, and airy inside. Its windows gave a wonderful view over the sea and the palm trees.

"It's so nice here, DP!" said Jack.

"It is, isn't it?" said DP. "And you remember our old friend Toilet Roll Angel?"

"Yes!" said Jack. "But I thought . . . I thought you were eaten by Toby-the-dog?"

"I was," said Toilet Roll Angel, who had a lovely singsong voice. "He tore me to pieces. All that's left of me Up There is a bit of wool, which you'll find under your second-largest present, if you look."

"But . . . I don't understand," said Jack. "You're *here*."

"The Alivened part of me, yes," said Toilet Roll Angel. "Mum loved me so much, I'm permitted to live forever on the Island of the Beloved."

"But then . . ." said Jack, turning to DP as a horrible thought struck him. "Does that mean . . . ? DP, Ambition told me a lorry ran over you!"

"I'm afraid . . . I'm afraid that's true, Jack," said DP quietly. "Grandpa put himself in danger Up There, trying to get me back, but a lorry came along and ran right over me. Grandpa saw me burst. All that's left of me now in the Land of the Living are a few beans and a bit of dirty cloth."

"But you're *here*," said Jack. "I can touch you! I can feel you! I can *smell* you!"

"Yes," said DP, leading Jack to a striped sofa and sitting down beside him, "you made that happen, by loving me so much. This island's a familiar place to me, you know. Things that are deeply loved drop straight down onto the Island of the Beloved whenever we're lost. We don't even have to pass through Mislaid! I've had friends here for years, because"—DP's old button eyes twinkled—"well, you *did* lose me quite a lot, you know, Jack."

"And does the Loser never come?" asked Jack.

"Never," said DP. "He isn't permitted to set foot on this island, and even if he did, he couldn't hurt us. Our humans' love has made us immortal."

"But if you were burst by the lorry, how can I take you home? CP promised I could have you back again!"

Now DP and Toilet Roll Angel exchanged very serious looks.

"Well . . . my brother's right," said DP. "You *can* take me back to the Land of the Living tonight, if you really want to. It's still Christmas Eve Up There: the night for miracles and lost causes. However—"

"CP, we did it!" cried Jack, turning to the Christmas Pig.

But the Christmas Pig wasn't there.

THE TRUTH

"CP? Christmas Pig? Where's he gone?" said Jack, looking around the room, then jumping off the sofa and hurrying to the window. "He dropped into the sea right behind me, didn't he? Oh no"—Jack gasped—"he didn't *drown*, did he? The water's not very deep—I thought he'd be safe!"

Now he came to think of it, Jack hadn't heard the splash of the Christmas Pig landing in the water behind him, he'd been far too interested in the sight of DP on the beach. Staring out of the window, he spotted something in the sky, something that looked like a gigantic bird flying away from the island, and realized it was Hope, returning to the mainland with the tapestry bundle still swinging beneath her.

"The Christmas Pig isn't allowed here, Jack," said Toilet Roll Angel in his singsong voice. "This is the place for Things that are deeply loved, up in the Land of the Living."

"But why's he flying away?" asked Jack, suddenly scared. "I've got to take him home. I promised to give him to Holly!"

"Jack," said DP, placing his trotter around Jack's shoulders again, "my brother always knew he wouldn't be able to return to the Land of the Living with you. Now that my body's been destroyed Up There, the only way I can leave the Land of the Lost is if a toy just like me makes up the Loser's numbers. The Christmas Pig decided to take my place. Every Thing knows that's how it works—but I never heard of a Thing volunteering to do it."

"Why would he do that?" whispered Jack. "*Why?*"

"He wanted to make you happy," said DP.

"He can't have done," said Jack in a very small voice. "I threw him at the wardrobe. I stamped on him. I—I tried to pull his head off."

"He understood why you did those things," said DP gently. "He was a Replacement, and Replacements, once Alivened, understand all about their owner from the very start. All that I know about you, he knows, and he's always loved you, just as much as I do."

"But—but why didn't he tell me?" whispered Jack as his eyes filled with tears again. "He pretended he could come back with me! He made me promise to give him to Holly!"

"He fibbed because he didn't want you to feel bad about what he was going to do," said DP. "CP's a modest pig. He knew your heart from the beginning and he believed he could never be to you what I am. So he decided to sacrifice himself, because your happiness was more important to him than his own."

"He should have told me!" said Jack. There was a lump as hard as a peach stone in his throat. "I thought we'd all be able to go home together! I thought I'd still see him! What will he do, when he gets back to the mainland?"

"Go to the Wastes," said DP quietly. "If I'm to go free, then the Christmas Pig must replace me in the Land of the Lost. As he's broken the law not once, but many times, any Thing that helps him now will surely be eaten. He always knew he'd have to face the Loser if he was to save me. I fear . . . I fear his time is short."

Jack turned back to the window, his eyes blurry with tears. Hope was now a tiny dot on the horizon.

"He should have told me!" Jack repeated as his tears spilled onto his cheeks. "It wasn't fair, not telling me!"

He remembered the Loser's searchlights sweeping across the Wastes and the dreadful story the Christmas Pig had told, of the Loser sucking out the Alivened part of a Thing.

It's what humans call death.

Jack stumbled back to DP's little striped sofa, sat down, and cried and cried. "I didn't want this!" he sobbed. "I never wanted him caught by the Loser!"

"I know you didn't, Jack," said DP, sitting down beside Jack and putting his trotters around him. The toilet roll angel sat on Jack's other side. He couldn't put an arm around Jack, because he didn't have any arms, but he sighed deeply and sadly.

Jack couldn't stop thinking about all that he and the Christmas Pig had gone through together. He remembered how the Christmas Pig had pretended not to like him very much, and realized that CP had done it to try and stop Jack from feeling guilty at this moment; he thought of how CP had saved them from Crusher by his quick thinking; and how his little snout had sunk beneath the green water in the City of the Missed before Jack rescued him. Now he realized that what he'd tasted last night in the tapestry had been CP's tears. While Jack had been so excited and happy about going to the Island of the Beloved, CP had been crying, because he'd known it was the last time he'd ever see Jack, and that when they reached the Island of the Beloved, they'd have to part forever.

All along, Jack had thought that if only he found DP, he'd be happy again, but he didn't feel happy at all. Now, when it was too late, he realized he'd come to love CP, not instead of DP, but quite separately, for his brave and good self. In that moment, Jack truly understood what it felt like to be Alivened, because he understood what he was meant to do.

"DP . . . I've got to rescue CP."

DP smiled, which made his snout wrinkle exactly the way CP's did. "I hoped you'd decide that, Jack. I'm glad."

"Will you—will you come with me?"

"You know I can't, Jack," said DP quietly, putting his old gray trotter on Jack's hand. "You can only take one of us home—but if you save CP, I'll be safe here, forever, on this beautiful island. It's a wonderful place and every day I think of you, and how grateful I am that you loved me."

Jack threw his arms around his oldest friend. He'd needed DP so much, and for such a long time, it seemed impossible that he could let him go. But then Jack thought of CP, and how much CP needed him now, so he let go of DP and said through his tears, "How will I get back to the Wastes? Hope's gone!"

For a moment, nobody said anything. Then Toilet Roll Angel piped up, "I think I know someone who can help. Follow me."

A FAMOUS FRIEND

Jack and DP followed Toilet Roll Angel out of the house facing the beach and off into the town that lay behind it. The buildings on the Island of the Beloved were all painted in ice-cream colors, the streets were very clean, and the other old toys—there didn't seem to be any other kind of Thing here—smiled and said hello as they passed. DP seemed to have lots of friends and there weren't any Loss Adjusters at all. They passed Christmas trees hung with shells and starfish, and shops selling buckets and spades, and a little market where you could buy beach balls and sunglasses. There was even a grooming parlor, where old toys could have splits in their fur sewn up and their eyes sewn back on, by dolls and teddies dressed as doctors.

"Here we are," said Toilet Roll Angel at last, pointing to a giant house made of wood, set in the very middle of town. The sign over the door said THE GROTTO. As Jack had shrunk to the size of DP, and the door was human-sized, he had no hope of being able to reach the doorbell.

"Who lives here?" he asked.

"You'll see," said Toilet Roll Angel. "You two will have to knock. I haven't got arms."

"Yes, I'm sorry about that," said Jack. "I was only four when I made you."

So Jack and DP hammered on the base of the door, but only Jack's knocks made any noise, because DP's trotters were too soft.

Jack could hear footsteps on the other side of the door: very loud footsteps, as though they were made by a giant. At last, the door creaked open.

There, towering above them, stood an old man with a snowy-white beard, dressed in a white undershirt and scarlet trousers.

"*Santa?*" gasped Jack. "What are *you* doing here?"

"Er—" said Santa, who for a moment seemed at a loss for what to say. "Well . . . Things deserve Christmas, too, you know, so I—I keep a holiday house here. But a living boy in the Land of the Lost? I never would have believed it—in fact, I didn't think it was possible!"

"It's only possible tonight," said Jack, "if it *is* still Christmas Eve, Up There?"

"Yes," said Santa, checking his watch. "Yes, there's still about an hour to go."

"Thank goodness. Then, please," said Jack, "could you help me rescue the Christmas Pig, so I can take him home? He's gone to the Wastes of the Unlamented, and I've got to save him from the Loser!"

"Ah," said Santa.

He stroked his beard for a moment or two, then sighed and

said, "That's something I can't promise, I'm afraid."

"Oh," said Jack, biting his lip to stop himself crying again.

"I'm not allowed to set foot on the mainland, you see," explained Santa. "The Loser and I—well, it's complicated. I give and he takes. Up There, I mostly have things my way. Here Below, he has his. I can fly you to the Wastes of the Unlamented in my sleigh, as long as I don't land, but then I'll have to leave you. Are you sure you wouldn't rather go home to your bed? It would be far safer and I could make that happen, easily."

"No," said Jack, shaking his head. "I've got to save the Christmas Pig."

"In that case," said Santa, "you're a very brave boy, and I shall ready my sleigh. Wait there."

Santa went back inside his house and closed the door, and Jack, DP, and Toilet Roll Angel waited in the sunshine for him to reappear. There was an odd feeling between them: Jack was still fighting back tears. There was so much he wanted to say to DP, yet he couldn't find the words.

At last, they heard the sound of hooves and jingling, and around the corner of the wooden house came Santa, now wearing his hat, jacket, and boots, leading the eight reindeer who were pulling his sleigh, which was piled high with presents. When they saw the sleigh, not to mention Santa with his hat and boots on, the toys passing by crowded around to watch him take off, and with so many Things watching, Jack found it even harder to put into words all he wanted to say to DP.

"Ready, Jack?" asked Santa.

"Yes," said Jack. "I—I just want to say goodbye." He turned to Toilet Roll Angel. "We'll miss you at the top of the tree."

"Thank you, Jack," said the angel in his singsong voice. "I'll miss being there."

Jack turned to DP. "I wish you could come home as well," he whispered.

For the very last time, DP put his trotters round Jack's neck and Jack breathed in his grubby smell of hiding places, and of the warm cave under the blankets, with a trace of Mum's perfume from when she kissed him good night.

"Losing is part of living," whispered DP into Jack's ear, his snout snuffling against Jack's hair. "But some of us live even though we're lost. That's what love does. I'll always be here, on the Island of the Beloved, and when you hug the Christmas Pig, you'll be hugging me, too, because we're twins, Jack, and everything he feels, I feel, too.

"But if you want to save him," DP went on, "you must be quick. Of all the Things on the Wastes, the Loser will most want to capture the Christmas Pig, as a warning to any Replacement who tries to cheat him in the future."

"Goodbye, DP," said Jack as he let go of his oldest friend.

Jack was so small now, Santa had to lift him up onto the sleigh.

"I'm glad I've seen where you live," Jack called down to DP, wiping away his tears again. "I always knew you loved the beach!"

"I do!" said DP, his button eyes as wet as Jack's. "Good luck, Jack, and give my brother my love! Thank him for what he tried to do! Tell him he's the best and bravest pig there ever was!"

THE SLEIGH RIDE

As the sleigh began to move, even more toys came rushing out of their houses to watch. The reindeer broke into a gallop and the warm wind whipped through Jack's hair. He looked back: DP and Toilet Roll Angel were growing smaller and smaller, and then, with a jingle of harness and a rush of hot air, the sleigh took off, and Jack watched the Island of the Beloved shrink below them. Soon, it was no more than a golden speck in the wide blue ocean.

Quite apart from Santa being much bigger than he was, because Jack was still the size of a toy, he was the most famous person Jack had ever met, which made him feel quite tongue-tied. Fortunately, Santa didn't need any encouragement to talk.

"After I've dropped you off, I'll have to go Up There and get busy delivering presents," he said, smiling down at Jack.

"How do you get all around the world and deliver so many toys in one night?" Jack asked. He'd often wondered this.

CHAPTER 53

"Ah," said Santa, his eyes twinkling, "that's a secret, I'm afraid, but it involves magic, as I expect you've guessed."

"I thought so," said Jack, nodding.

"You, of course, asked for a new bike," said Santa.

"Yes," said Jack. "But I don't really care about the bike, as long as I get the Christmas Pig back."

"Well, if you *do* manage to rescue him, be sure to take him for a ride," said Santa. "He's a pig who greatly enjoys bike rides, though he doesn't know it yet, being so new."

"That makes sense," said Jack, imagining pedaling fast down his street, with the Christmas Pig tucked down the front of his hoodie, CP's head poking out of the top. "He's quite a *daring* pig, isn't he?"

"Very daring," agreed Santa, "to defy the Loser as he has."

"Where did the Loser come from?" asked Jack.

"That," said Santa, no longer smiling, "is a very good question. Nobody knows for sure. Some say he was created by people, that there is so much greed and cruelty Up There that some of it oozed down here, where it began kidnapping Things to help it make a body. Others say the Loser's been here since the dawn of time, a kind of monster who's so envious of humans and all the clever things they create, he steals whatever he can. More than anything else, he craves Things that are valued and loved, like those on the Island of the Beloved, but he can't touch them, which makes him very angry. Now, poke around in the presents at the back there, Jack, and grab yourself something warm to wear."

Jack felt the presents to find one that was squashy and at last unearthed a teddy wearing a sweater that fit him perfectly. He was glad of it, because a few minutes later the warm air began to turn chillier. The painted sky above them turned slowly from bright blue to gray. The sun disappeared behind clouds, and soon snow was whirling down on Jack again.

They flew on, the reindeer's harness jingling, the icy air numbing Jack's face. His thoughts were full of CP, who'd surely have reached the Wastes of the Unlamented by now. He'd be wandering there, missing Jack, loving Jack, but believing that Jack had already returned to the Land of the Living, too happy with DP to care what had become of his Replacement.

RETURN TO THE WASTES

At last, when the sky had turned from gray to black, and the snow was falling so thickly that it coated Santa's beard and Jack's eyelashes, they spotted the lights of the City of the Missed. They flew over the golden roof of Power's palace, the canals reflecting Santa's sleigh and the flying reindeer, and soon they were soaring over the wide, dark Wastes.

Santa now hung a golden lantern on a hook, to shed some light on the ground below. Jack looked around, hoping to see the Christmas Pig. The shadow of the sleigh rippled over the snowy, stony ground, but there was no sign of any Thing until they glimpsed a small red spot of wandering light.

"Bad habits," Jack told Santa, pointing to the little group of roaming body parts, which still included a mouth smoking a cigarette. "They aren't very nice . . . I think the Loser's caught a few of them," added Jack, turning back to look at the Bad Habits as the sleigh flew on. "There were more when we met them before."

They continued to skim as low over the Wastes as Santa dared, scanning the barren landscape for CP, but Jack couldn't see him anywhere. Now an awful fear gripped his heart: Was he too late? Had CP been caught already?

"Compass!" cried Jack suddenly as the swinging light of the lantern illuminated her round brass body, which was bowling along as fast as ever. "Santa, let me ask Compass if she's seen CP!"

Santa turned the sleigh around and they doubled back to where Compass stood staring at the sight of them.

"*Santa!*" she cried.

"That's me," said Santa, smiling. "Glad to see you're still with us, Compass!"

"Oh, you know 'ow much I enjoy the chase," she said, spinning to watch them as they circled her. "But what're you two doing 'ere?"

"I've come to find the Christmas Pig," called Jack. "Have you seen him?"

At that, Compass's pointer swung suddenly south, giving her a very sad look.

"Well . . . yes, Pajama Boy, I have," she said.

"Where is he?" called Jack, who was starting to get dizzy, because the sleigh was flying in such tight circles.

"I'm afraid," said Compass, "'e was caught, 'alf an hour ago. 'E didn't even run. I shouted at 'im to scarper, but 'e just stood there, waiting for the Loser to snatch 'im up."

CHAPTER 54

"Oh no," Jack whispered.

It was all his fault. He ought to have gotten there sooner, but he'd wasted time deciding what to do, and now . . .

"So he's in the Loser's Lair?" called Santa.

"'E's there if 'e's anywhere," said Compass, "but 'e might already 'ave been eaten. The Loser was delighted to get 'is 'ands on 'im. Never seen 'im so 'appy!"

"Compass, d'you know where the Loser's Lair is?" called Jack.

"'Course I do," said Compass.

"Will you take me there?"

"You want to go to the Loser's Lair?" said Compass in astonishment.

"Yes," said Jack, preparing to jump. "CP's my pig and if he's still Alivened, I'm taking him home!"

"Jack," said Santa as Jack got ready to jump, "if I can, I'll give you more help later—there might be something I can do for you, Up There. In the meantime, be very careful. The Loser would like nothing better than to catch a living boy!"

"I'll be careful," promised Jack. "Goodbye, Santa, thank you very much!"

With that, Jack eased himself off the sleigh's seat and jumped down onto the Wastes.

He fell into a clump of thistles he hadn't spotted in the darkness, and although it was an uncomfortable, prickly landing, it was better than landing on the sharp flints and stones.

"Goodbye, Jack. Good luck!" called Santa, and he flew away

on his sleigh, the golden lantern growing smaller and smaller until it disappeared.

Compass was staring at Jack in amazement.

"*What* did Santa just call you?" She rolled a little closer. "A *living boy?*"

"Yes," said Jack. "I'm human. I came down here to find DP, but he's happy on the Island of the Beloved. Now I want to save the Christmas Pig. Please take me to the Loser's Lair, if you know the way."

Compass stared at Jack for a moment longer, then her voice rang out across the Wastes, "They'll talk of this for centuries! The living boy 'oo walked into the Loser's Lair to find 'is pig and . . . Well, we don't know 'ow the story ends, do we?"

"Not yet," said Jack, "but please, if you know the way, show me!"

Compass set off and Jack ran after her across the frozen ground, and the snow fell thick and fast in their faces.

Part Eight

THE LOSER'S LAIR

THE CRATER

"It's not too far, don't worry!" said Compass, her brass case clattering over the stones.

Even so, Jack soon had a stitch again and his sore feet were frozen, but he didn't care at all. All he could think about was CP, who'd stood and let the Loser scoop him up, because he thought Jack didn't love him.

They'd only run a short way when they saw a fiery red glow on the horizon, which grew wider and brighter as they approached.

"It's right ahead," said Compass. "See that fire? The Loser lives in an 'ole in the middle of a crater, and 'e burns a fire all year round. After 'e's sucked out the Alivened part of a Thing, and taken what 'e wants of their bodies, 'e burns up the rest in the flames."

Jack felt a shiver of fear, but didn't slow down. He had to save CP if he could: there was no turning back.

The closer to the Loser's Lair they approached, the bigger and brighter the fiery glow became, and at last the ground began to slope downward. Jack could see a wide hole in the middle of the crater, like a volcano, from which acrid black smoke was issuing. He looked up at the sky above the Loser's Lair. There were no finding holes here at all.

"Stop, Compass," Jack panted, coming to a halt. "I'll go on alone now."

"Nonsense," said Compass excitedly. "I've never been in the Loser's Lair before. What a thrill! What an adventure! You know what my motto is?"

"Was it something about a radish?" asked Jack, who couldn't quite remember.

"That was a moral," said Compass. "I meant, 'socks in the north and umbrellas for best, but when it's all going south, take a friend.' You can't meet the Loser alone!"

"I can, Compass," Jack told her. "I must. You're too important to lose. Things need a hero out here on the Wastes, and you're the only one clever and brave enough to survive."

"What—what a nice fing to say," said Compass. "Fings never pay me compliments. They're usually running away so fast, they forget."

"Well, I won't forget you, whatever happens," said Jack. "Goodbye, Compass, and thank you for everything."

And he ran down the slope toward the hole in the ground, turning back just once to wave while he knew Compass could still see him.

Jack descended the steep slope, sliding and stumbling on loose rocks and stones. He went as fast as he dared, half-blinded by the fire and smoke coming from the hole in the middle of the crater, and soon his pajamas had dried out completely in the heat, and he began to cough from the thick black smoke, which didn't smell like a wood bonfire, but reeked of burning plastic, fabric, and foam.

And then, just when Jack was wondering how much farther he'd have to go, his feet now burning on the hot rubble, he slid on loose pebbles, and unable to stop, found himself tumbling into the hole. Down he fell through the smoke into an underground lair, and for a few seconds, he was sure he was going to land in the flames, and that he'd never see Mum or CP again.

THE LOSER'S LAIR

By great good fortune, Jack missed the fire and fell instead onto a hot, springy, soft mound right beside it. It was a few moments before Jack realized he was lying on stuffing and shreds of fabric that the Loser had discarded from the Things he'd eaten. It was smoking and smoldering because it lay so close to the flames. Jack crawled as fast as he could toward a distant stone wall, slipping and sliding over the heaps of fluff and burned material, until he'd reached the side of the underground hole.

It was then that he heard the moans and screams which had been drowned out by the crackling of the enormous fire while he'd lain beside it. Jack screwed up his eyes and looked around.

The Loser's Lair was a gigantic underground cavern, in the middle of which burned the huge fire. Cages hung all over the walls, all of them crammed with the Things the Loser hadn't yet eaten, and it was the cries of some of these imprisoned Things he could hear, although not all of them were screaming. Many were simply huddled at the bottom of their cages, silent and sad, knowing that their end had almost come. They were cheap, ugly Things, most of them: made and lost in their millions, unwanted, unloved, existing only to fill space for a while until they were sucked down below into the Land of the Lost.

And then there was the Loser.

He was so gigantic that—for a moment or two—Jack, who was focused on the cages, hadn't realized he was there, but had taken his enormous body for another pile of junk. The Loser was crouching on the opposite side of the fire to Jack, his horrible head scraping the top of his lair, as it had scraped the wooden sky on the Wastes. His searchlight eyes weren't turned on: he didn't need them here, because the fire burned so brightly, casting flickering shadows onto the walls. The Loser's blank glass eyes reflected the dancing flames, which also illuminated the glittering shell of his body. Evidently the Loser kept only the hardest parts of dead Things: steel, plastic, glass, and stone, which gave him the look of a dreadful robot. At this moment, he was feasting on a handful of old forks, and bits of them flew from his mouth as he crunched them up with his glittering fangs, which appeared to be as hard as diamonds.

The Loser hadn't noticed Jack fall into his lair because Jack had fallen on the opposite side of the fire and been hidden by the thick black smoke. Now Jack looked frantically around at all the cages, trying to spot the Christmas Pig, and hoping against hope that he hadn't already been torn to shreds, his belly beans and stuffing lost in the mounds below.

But Jack couldn't see a single cuddly toy: only small plastic playthings that came free with meals, and old magazines, and chargers for gadgets that no longer worked; objects lost without regret and never missed. Jack's fear that he was too late mounted with every second.

And then, suddenly, Jack spotted him. CP was standing inside one of the very highest cages on the wall, gripping the bars with his little trotters and watching the Loser eat the old forks. With him was Broken Angel, who was slumped in a corner of the cage, her one remaining hand over her shattered face. CP was shabby now, after all his adventures with Jack: no longer plush and pink, but dirty, greenish, and with lopsided ears.

"I'm coming, CP," whispered Jack, struggling to his feet.

Then the Loser chomped down the last bits of twisted metal and spoke, his voice echoing around the cavern. "*Now* are you afraid, Pig?"

His voice was the most terrible Jack had ever heard. It was like the scream of brakes, high and pained, and it made Jack think that the Loser must be suffering almost as much as the Things waiting for their death.

CP answered, in his dear familiar voice, "No. I told you. I have nothing left to lose, which makes a Thing brave. Eat me whenever you like. It doesn't matter to me anymore."

"You think losing the boy is worse than being torn apart?" said the Loser, in his screeching voice. "Worse than returning to nothingness, to feeling nothing, to *being* nothing?"

"Feeling nothing would be better than what I feel now," said the pig.

"Don't say that!" whispered Jack, even though he knew the Christmas Pig couldn't hear him.

The Loser struggled onto the metal points that served him for feet.

"You will fear me before you die," he promised. He tore the lock off a crowded cage right next to the one holding the Christmas Pig and Broken Angel, and scooped out fifty twisty plastic straws in gaudy colors, a cheap, flimsy kite, and an ugly glass vase with knobs and twirls all over it. Jack heard their screams of protest as the Loser sank back into a crouch, opened his wide metal mouth, and dropped the Things into it one by one.

In desperation, Jack looked around for a way to reach the Christmas Pig. The walls were rough and craggy, and he thought he might be able to find enough toeholds to climb them if he tried, so he reached up, found cracks where he could grip, then began to pull himself upward.

It was slow going. The rock burned beneath his fingers and toes, and behind him he could hear the crackle of the fire and the grinding of the Loser's jaws as he ate his way through plastic and glass.

At last, Jack reached the same level as the topmost cages. It was harder to grip the hot rock up here, and he was worried the poor Things inside the cages might notice him and shout out in surprise, alerting the Loser to the fact that Jack was there. However, most were shielding their eyes, trying not to watch the Loser, who was now picking sharp fragments of glass out of his teeth and attaching them to his shell, which he did by licking them with his horrible black rubber tongue, which seemed to be coated in some kind of glue, then sticking them down on top of the cogs and lids already there.

Jack began to walk across the tops of the cages, jumping from one to the next. The bars were hot beneath his soles, but a new problem struck him as he approached the Christmas Pig, whose little black eyes were still fixed unblinkingly on the Loser. All the cages had heavy padlocks dangling from them, and the one hanging from CP's was the biggest of all.

At last, Jack managed to jump onto the cage holding the Christmas Pig and Broken Angel. "CP," he whispered. "CP, it's me. Look up here."

CP looked up, and for a moment or two, he stood frozen, his little black eyes wide with astonishment, and Broken Angel uncovered her poor half-eaten face and stared up at Jack, too.

"Jack!" gasped the Christmas Pig. "What—what are you—?"

"I've come to rescue you—both of you!" said Jack, crawling across the cage roof to grasp hold of the giant padlock. "You two belong to me, and I'm taking you home!"

"But . . . what about DP?"

"We've said goodbye properly now," said Jack, tugging at the padlock, which remained shut. "He wanted me to do this. I'm going to get you out!"

But he couldn't open the padlock.

"Jack—I don't understand—you wanted DP so much!"

"I thought I needed him," said Jack. "But you need me more."

"You've got to get out of here! There's nothing in the whole of the Land of the Lost that the Loser would like better than to eat a living boy! You'd be the greatest prize he ever caught!"

"I'm not leaving without you," said Jack, still trying to break the padlock, but it wouldn't shift.

"It's too late!" said the Christmas Pig, his tears now trickling down his face. "Jack, there are only a few minutes until Christmas Day—you've got to get yourself under a finding hole! There's no hope for us, but you can still escape!"

But before Jack could reply, the Loser let out the loudest, most terrifying screech Jack had ever heard. His eyes blazed white again as he rose up on his pointed metal feet. Jack, the Christmas Pig, and Broken Angel were caught, transfixed, in their powerful beams.

The Loser had spotted the living boy.

THE LAST HOPE

"What is this I spy?" said the Loser, in his awful screeching voice. "A bit of Surplus very different to any I've caught before!"

Jack thrust his hand down between the bars of the cage and seized one of the Christmas Pig's trotters. The broken angel caught hold of CP's other trotter, and the threesome held tightly to one another as the Loser picked his way slowly across the cavern toward them, scattering bits of dead Things with his pointed steel feet. All around the walls, the Things in the cages moaned and gasped, because they'd realized what was happening, and knew that Jack, the Christmas Pig, and Broken Angel would be going into the Loser's mouth next.

"I knew you'd come. Tell me, child," said the Loser, "what makes humans love Things so much?"

The Loser's breath swept over Jack like a hot, foul wind. It smelled as though every rubbish heap in the world was lying in his stomach, of dust, decay, and rotting cloth, of battery acid and burning rubber, of the end of all man-made Things.

"We don't love all Things," said Jack in a shaking voice. "Only very special ones."

"And what," said the Loser, moving closer, his gigantic head bigger than Jack's entire body, his searchlight eyes so bright that Jack could barely look at him, "makes a filthy, cheap pig worth loving?"

"He's the best and bravest pig in the world, that's what," said Jack fiercely.

"You—you love me?" whispered the Christmas Pig.

Jack gripped his trotter more tightly than ever as he said, "Yes, I do!"

"But—but DP!"

"You can love more than one Thing!" said Jack. Turning back to the Loser he said, "Let CP go, and Broken Angel, too! They don't deserve eating. They've never hurt anyone, they've never done anything wrong! Let them come home with me!"

The Loser threw back his head, opened his horrid mouth wide to reveal his huge rubber tongue, lying like a thick black eel between glittering fangs, and laughed. Then he turned his bright, blinding eyes back on Jack and screamed, "Has nobody explained to you what I am, boy? I take, and take, and take again! Christmas Eve is almost over"—the Loser was moving closer, his awful rough diamond teeth glinting in the red light of the fire, his breath a disgusting blast—"and on the last stroke of midnight, you'll be trapped here forever, with no hope of return. Then I shall swallow you, and perhaps then I'll love Things as much as people do!"

All around the walls, the cheap and unloved Things wailed and shivered and sobbed in their cages. "Not the boy! *Not the boy!*"

"You're pleading for him?" jeered the Loser, his searchlight eyes sweeping the cages where the poor cheap Things were cowering. "Humans made you, cast you aside, and forgot you—it's all their fault you were sent to the Wastes! You're cheap and you're ugly, and your owners thought you worthless! You should be glad to watch a human die, before I chew you to pieces!"

But Jack had just had an idea. He knew it might be too late, but it was the only thing he could think of that might work. "Listen!" he shouted to all the Things in their cages, while he still clung to the Christmas Pig's trotter. "I'm human and I care about you! You aren't garbage to me, and I know how to get you out of here!"

And with these words, the giant padlock on the Christmas Pig's cage shattered. The Things all around the cavern walls gasped in shock and then, one by one, all around the cavern, more padlocks began to burst apart, then more, then even more. The Loser shrieked in rage and shock, but Jack knew what had happened. He'd given the Things hope, which no lock can contain. Now a few of the bravest began clambering out of their cages, helping one another as they went.

"There's a way out for all of you, I promise!" shouted Jack to all the shivering Things still too scared to leave their prisons. "You've just got to believe!"

"Get back!" shrieked the Loser, enraged to see the Things

escaping. "He's lying! Get back! BACK! I shall eat all those who climb out first!"

"I'm not lying!" Jack shouted. "If everyone hopes and believes—"

And then something extraordinary happened—something simply magnificent. It could only have happened on the night for miracles and lost causes, and only then because Jack had refused to give up hope, because nothing can be lost for good until all hope has gone . . .

Up in the dark wooden sky above the Loser's Lair, where there'd been no finding holes at all, the sky cracked. The monstrous Loser looked up at the sound of the sky breaking open and screamed in fury. A hole had appeared there, but it wasn't dark, like an ordinary finding hole. Sparkling light was whooshing around inside it, as though it contained moving magic, and Jack knew what the magic was, because once, long ago, when he was only three years old, he'd imagined DP whooshing around inside a hole just like that, on a magical bicycle.

"This is your way back to the Land of the Living!" he cried. "Keep hoping!"

The hole grew larger and larger. It was wide and golden, and then the real magic happened: instead of dropping a single shaft of golden light, and saving one Thing, the sparkling, circling light descended in a spiral and whooshed up inside it hundreds and hundreds of astonished, delighted Things. Out of their dirty cages they rose, the tin and the cardboard, the wooden, the paper, and the plastic, each of them laughing as they were drawn into the sparkling, whirling cyclone. The furious, bewildered Loser didn't

understand what was happening, and though he spun around trying to catch them, they slid through his long steel fingers and up toward the new hole their hope had made in the ceiling.

"They're going to be recycled!" Jack shouted as the monstrous creature tried to catch the Things rising so fast beyond his grip. "They'll be made new, Up There, and live again!"

"No!" shrieked the Loser, wild with rage. "People can't have them! They're mine, they're mine, they belong to me—"

From somewhere up above the glittering hole where the saved Things were disappearing, there came the chimes of a distant clock. It was midnight in the Land of the Living. Christmas Eve was finally ending.

"If I can't have them," screamed the enraged Loser, "I'll have *you*!"

The Loser reached out his clawlike hands, with the fingers as long as steel girders, and Jack heard the chimes, and knew that hope wouldn't be enough now. The only comfort left in the world was the feel of the pig's trotter in his hand and he closed his eyes as the Loser's searchlight eyes grew nearer and brighter.

And then he felt himself

falling . . .

falling . . .

falling . . .

Part Nine
HOME

FOUND

The smell of the Loser's breath had vanished. Still Jack fell, eyes tight shut, clutching the Christmas Pig's trotter, and he was scraped by sharp branches that smelled of pine, and down, down, down they fell until Jack felt ground beneath him. A distant voice was calling his name, a voice he knew.

"Hope?" he murmured.

A door opened.

"Jack?" said the voice, and then, "Jack! What are you doing under the tree? We've been looking for you everywhere!"

Jack opened his eyes. He was curled up on the floor beneath the Christmas tree at home, in the middle of all the presents, the tree lights gleaming in the darkness above him. Pine needles were scattered all around him, and he'd returned to his normal size. The teddy bear–sized sweater had burst off him and now lay beside him in a tiny knitted ball. One hand was still holding the trotter of the Christmas Pig and there, her undamaged hand lying stretched out on the floor touching the Christmas Pig's other trotter, was Broken Angel.

"Brendan, I've found him!" called Mum, kneeling to look at Jack through the branches. "What are you doing under there, Jack? I went into your bedroom to give you a kiss and you'd gone. I was worried sick!"

She reached out a hand, and Jack crawled out from under the tree with CP in one hand and the broken angel in the other, and Mum pulled him into a hug and Jack hugged her back. It felt wonderful to be home again.

"I'm so sorry about DP," Mum whispered. "Grandpa told me what happened. When I didn't find you in bed, I thought you might have sneaked out to try and find him and I—"

"I *did* go to look for DP!" said Jack. "And I was just nearly eaten by the Loser, and I escaped, I don't know how—"

But then Jack spotted the shiny new bike with a big red ribbon on it, which was leaning up against the wall beside the tree, its handlebars touching the branches, and he pulled free of Mum to point at it.

"*That's* how! Santa *said* he might be able to help me later! He knocked the angel loose!"

"What?" said Mum, confused.

Jack showed Mum the chewed-up angel with her bent wing.

"She was caught in the branches at the back of the tree, see? But when Santa put my new bike there, he wobbled the tree on purpose and knocked her free! So she wasn't lost anymore and she pulled me and the Christmas Pig with her, back into the Land of the Living!"

"Jack, *what* are you talking about?" said Mum, half laughing, half-worried. Brendan now hurried into the room and clapped his hand over his heart.

"Thank goodness for that," he said, looking at Jack. "We thought you were lost, buddy!"

"I *was*!" said Jack as Holly entered the room behind Brendan. Her eyes were still puffy, because she'd been crying so much, but she gave a huge gasp of relief when she saw Jack alive and well beside the Christmas tree.

"I was in the Land of the Lost!" Jack told them all. "Me and CP went there together! I found DP and he's happy—I always *knew* he liked the beach—and I met so many different Things—and there are all these different cities and the Loser nearly got me, but then Broken Angel saved us—we've got to keep her!" said Jack, thrusting the mangled angel under Mum's nose.

"Well," said Mum with a little laugh, as she took the angel from him, "she does look as though she belongs to this family, all right. I think she'd have been a bit grand for us before Toby-the-dog got her."

"You can bandage her up, can't you?" said Jack. "Like you did to DP, when he had his new eyes sewn on?"

"Of course," said Mum. Then she sniffed and said, "Why do you smell of smoke? And why are your pajamas so muddy?"

"Oh, the smell's the Loser's fire and the mud's from where Blue Bunny hugged me," said Jack. "It's hard to keep clean in the Land of the Lost."

"Well, I don't know about all that, but that pig definitely needs a wash."

CHAPTER 58

"Not yet," said Jack, hugging the Christmas Pig to his chest. "He's quite scared of water at the moment, because he can't swim. That's why he's green. He nearly drowned in a canal. I'll need to explain to him about the washing machine before you put him in it, or he'll be really frightened. Anyway, I want to take him on a ride on my new bike before that. He likes bike rides. Santa told me."

"That was quite some dream you had," said Mum. "And you're not supposed to have seen that bike yet. It isn't Christmas Day."

"Actually," said Brendan, checking his watch, "it is. It's one minute past midnight."

"I'm hungry," said Jack. "I've been away three whole nights, and I couldn't eat the food in the Land of the Lost, because that would have proved I was a living boy. You don't believe me." Jack looked from Mum's face to Brendan's. They were both smiling in that annoying way grown-ups have, when they think they know better than you do what happened, even though you were there, and saw it all.

"Why don't I make some hot chocolate?" said Mum, still smiling. She carried Broken Angel out of the room. Brendan turned on the electric fire and went to help her in the kitchen, leaving Holly and Jack alone.

"*I* believe you were in the Land of the Lost," said Holly in a hoarse voice. "I do, Jack. And I'm glad you saw DP and that he's happy. And I'm sorry—so, so sorry—I threw him out of the car window."

"Well . . . it's all right," said Jack. "He's living in a nice little house on the beach with Toilet Roll Angel now. And I've got CP.

DP says he's the best and bravest pig there ever was, and he's right."

"What else happened, while you were in the Land of the Lost?" Holly asked, and she and Jack sat down by the fire, and Jack told Holly all about Disposable and Sheriff Specs, about Lunch Box and Inhaler, about Bother-It's-Gone, Addie, and Poem, about their long journey across the Wastes of the Unlamented, Compass, Blue Bunny, the strange Things he'd met in the City of the Missed, and their escape from the Loser's Lair.

"I know I've been horrible to you, Jack," said Holly, when at last he paused for breath. "And I promise I won't bully you, not ever again."

"I believe you," said Jack, remembering Bullyboss, whom he hadn't mentioned. CP was sitting on Jack's knee, so he could be warmed by the fire, too. "But I think you should stop doing gymnastics. I know you're not enjoying it anymore and you'd rather do music."

"How—*how* did you know that?" said Holly, amazed. "I haven't told *anyone*!"

"You find things out, in the Land of the Lost," said Jack wisely.

"I always thought I wanted to go to the Olympics," said Holly, looking into the fire, "but I really don't anymore. I'd rather see my friends at weekends, instead of practicing, practicing all the time."

"There's nothing wrong with losing an ambition," said Jack. "I met a lost ambition Down There, you know. She was horrible, but I'm sure you can get a nice new one."

"I'd like to learn the guitar," said Holly.

"Well, that's lucky," said Brendan, who'd come back into the room holding two big mugs of hot chocolate. "Judy and I have just agreed you can open one present each before you go back to bed. Holly, I think you should unwrap that big one, in the gold paper."

Jack untied the red ribbon on his new bike and showed the Christmas Pig all the features that made it such a particularly good one, while Holly tore the paper off her biggest present, to reveal a shiny black guitar. Then, while Holly was learning her first chord, Brendan helped Jack adjust the seat on his bike and Mum reappeared holding Broken Angel.

She'd wound a little strip of gauze around the angel's face to hide the bit that was missing, unbent her wing, and bandaged up her handless arm. Then Brendan, who was tallest, took the angel and placed her back at the top of the tree where she smiled down upon them all as proudly as if she'd been meant to be bandaged up all along.

"I like her," said Mum. "She looks kind, doesn't she? All right, you two, it's time for bed if you've finished that chocolate. We'll be up in a few hours, anyway."

So Jack and Holly climbed the stairs and said a friendly good night to each other on the landing. Then Holly disappeared into the spare room, and Mum came into Jack's room to kiss him good night.

None of the Things there were talking or moving anymore, and none of them had eyes or arms except those that had always had them. Jack snuggled up beneath his duvet and Mum kissed him, and then the Christmas Pig. She turned out the light and closed the door.

Jack lay cuddled up in bed breathing in CP's smell, which was of canal water and smoke, with a tiny trace of Mum's perfume. He'd have to go in the washing machine soon, but Jack knew he'd eventually come to smell of home, and of the warm cave under Jack's blankets.

"Good night, CP," whispered Jack. "Merry Christmas."

Exhausted from his adventures, Jack fell asleep almost at once.

It was no longer Christmas Eve, the night for miracles and lost causes, yet two little trotters hugged the sleeping boy in the darkness.

"Good night, Jack," whispered the little pig, whose tears of happiness were trickling down onto the pillow. "Merry Christmas to you, too!"

ACKNOWLEDGMENTS

The Christmas Pig, which has been years in the writing, lies very close to my heart. Setting it free at last has been a joyful and cathartic experience.

A huge debt of gratitude is owed to Aine Kiely, one of my oldest and dearest friends, who served as my personal Compass when she reminded me in a bleak moment a few years ago that Christmas comes every single year, thereby saving my sanity. It's thanks to Aine that I've loved writing this book as much as I have.

Ruth Alltimes was the perfect editor to work with on this project. Her insight, enthusiasm, and empathy made the editing process a total delight. I'm also immensely grateful to Emily Clement at Scholastic for her contributions, all of which improved the story.

My gratitude as ever to my friend and agent, Neil Blair, and to all at The Blair Partnership who've been involved in *The Christmas Pig*.

Massive thanks to my indispensable management team, Nicky Stonehill, Rebecca Salt, and Mark Hutchinson, for letting me tell them the whole story over lunch. Limit me to two glasses in future.

Without Fiona Shapcott, Di Brooks, Angela Milne, and Simon Brown, I'd probably still be writing the last book but one. Thank you for everything you do.

Jim Field was the perfect illustrator for this project. I cannot thank him enough for capturing Jack, the two pigs, and the Land of the Lost so beautifully. I regularly gasped on seeing his pictures, because they so exactly matched what I was seeing in my mind's eye.

Finally, and most importantly, thank you to my family. *The Christmas Pig* was truly Alivened back when five Murrays were sitting on a sandy beach, and I explained the Land of the Lost to you. Your enthusiasm, interest, and logic questions (Dec) kept me writing. All that remains to say is that any resemblance between the Things in these pages and the Things our family may have lost or found is, of course, entirely intentional.

J.K. ROWLING is the author of the seven Harry Potter books, which have sold over 500 million copies, been translated into over 80 languages, and made into eight blockbuster films. She also wrote three short series companion volumes for charity, including *Fantastic Beasts and Where to Find Them*, which later became the inspiration for a new series of films. Harry's story as a grown-up was later continued in a stage play, *Harry Potter and the Cursed Child*, which J.K. Rowling wrote with playwright Jack Thorne and director John Tiffany.

In 2020, she returned to publishing for younger children with the fairy tale *The Ickabog*, which she initially published for free online for children in lockdown, later donating all her book royalties to her charitable trust, Volant, to help vulnerable groups affected by the COVID-19 pandemic.

J.K. Rowling has received many awards and honors for her writing, including for her detective series written under the name Robert Galbraith. She supports a wide number of humanitarian causes through Volant, and is the founder of the international children's care reform charity Lumos.

For as long as she can remember, J.K. Rowling wanted to be a writer, and is at her happiest in a room, making things up. She lives in Scotland with her family.

To find out more about J.K. Rowling, visit jkrowlingstories.com.

JIM FIELD is an award-winning illustrator, character designer, and animation director. He has worked on a wide variety of projects, from music videos and title sequences to advertising and books.

His first picture book, *Cats Ahoy!*, won the Booktrust Roald Dahl Funny Prize and was nominated for the Kate Greenaway Medal. Since then, he has illustrated a string of bestselling, multi-award-winning children's books, including *Frog on a Log?* and *The Lion Inside*, as well as young fiction series Rabbit & Bear, middle-grade novels by David Baddiel, and his debut author-illustrator picture book, *Monsieur Roscoe on Vacation*, a bilingual book that introduces first French words. He grew up in Farnborough, UK, worked in London, and now lives in Paris with his wife and young daughter.